CHRISTMAS
with the
DEAD

Short Story by

Joe R. Lansdale

Screenplay by

Keith Lansdale

Encyclopocalypse Publications
www.encyclopocalypse.com

Christmas with the Dead - The Short Story
Copyright © 2010 by Joe R. Lansdale

Christmas with the Dead - The Screenplay
Copyright © 2012 by Joe R. Lansdale

Foreword
Copyright © 2024 by T.L. Lankford

All rights reserved.

ISBN: 978-1-960721-99-0

Cover Design and Formatting by Sean Duregger
Original Poster and DVD Artwork used by permission
Interior design and formatting by Mark Alan Miller and Sean
Duregger

The characters and events in this book are fictitious. Any
similarity to real persons, living, dead or undead is coincidental
and not intended by the author.

No part of this book may be reproduced in any form or by any
electronic or mechanical means, including information storage
and retrieval systems, without permission in writing from the
publisher, except by a reviewer who may quote brief passages in a
review.

CONTENTS

FOREWORD
T.L. LANKFORD

The phone rang at 3 a.m.. It was famed writer Joe R. Lansdale calling.

"What are you doing next month?"

"No plans."

"How about the month after?"

"Nada."

"And the month after that?"

"I got nothing."

"Can you come to Nacogdoches and make a movie for me?"

"Sure."

Joe R. Lansdale is a great writer. He's an even better friend. When he asks me to do something I say yes. Even if it's something I don't like to do anymore. Which is direct movies. I swore it off in the mid-90s after a friend of mine was killed on a set (not one of my sets, but not the first friend I lost to a movie set either) and then I made a movie where two people in two separate incidents might have died if things had gone just a little more wrong. A year at AFI pulling novices out of pools of water before they hit power switches and catching equipment rolling off the back of trucks before it could crush someone was enough to get me to swear off set work for a long time. Sets are dangerous places and I just didn't want to be personally responsible for so many lives. I decided to give novel writing a shot. That kept me busy for a decade or more.

I drifted back to filmmaking a bit when I started making documentaries and promotional films for Michael Connelly. But these were small productions with not as many moving parts as full scale feature films. Not as dangerous an environment. Not as big a responsibility. What Joe wanted me to do now was to take over a production being made with the help of a filmmaking class at Stephen F. Austin University. It was their "Summer Project" that would help many of the class graduate. So we were going to make a feature length film with very limited resources and, for the most part, a student crew, during a record heatwave in the heart of a Texas summer.

Sounds like fun, right?

It was. For the most part.

Joe had written a short story called *Christmas with the Dead*. His son Keith had turned it into a screenplay. We gathered a cast and workshopped it for about a month. (When you work with Lansdales, every word and comma mean something.) Then we shot the hell out of it. Sweating and grunting like a bunch of prisoners on a chain gang clearing brush in the everglades. It was a rare day when no member of the cast or crew didn't fall victim to the heat. We had one day where half of them went down to the ground, including the set paramedic.

"Lee, the medic passed out. He's laying on the floor of the auto dealership."

"Please water him regularly."

You ever wait six hours for forty people to have zombie make-up applied to their faces only to watch them eat most of it along with their barbecued chicken at dinner before you could shoot one shot of them?

I have.

You ever been so hot that you drank 20 gallons of water throughout the day and never took a leak until the middle of the night, then stood for more than an hour over the toilet as it all made an escape for the sea, napping against a cupboard as the stream continued for what seemed like eternity?

I have.

You ever pass out in the middle of a swimming pool at 4 a.m. only to be woken up by two bats trying to make babies in your hair?

I have.

These are the adventures of filmmaking that make the job so special.

Nacogdoches is a small, college town. It is famous for being the place the Marx Brothers found their act, with the help of a runaway mule. (Look it up!) It is also a town filled with very helpful people. We could not have made this movie without their generous aid. Everyone was very welcoming to this production. People provided locations for free or at a big discount. Others came out and played zombies in the heat. Some even played zombies IN heat. Everywhere I turned I saw nice people doing nice things.

Did anyone misbehave? Of course! But you won't hear about that from me. Not here, at least.

There were times where I thought the production would never end. And for some, it hasn't. I still get calls late into the night from people who worked on this movie and want to know where I hid their water bottles.

I drank them, you fools!

Seriously, though, I'd like to thank the cast and crew as well as all of Nacogdoches for helping us make this little film. It's tiny in budget, but I think it fights above its weight class. I'd also like to express my love and admiration for the Lansdales - Joe, Keith, Kasey, and Karen - who have made the world around them a much more vibrant place. It's been an honor and privilege to be their friend.

-Terrill Lee Lankford
Sherman Oaks, California
September 8, 2024

CHRISTMAS with the DEAD

Short Story by
Joe R. Lansdale

It was a foolish thing to do, and Calvin had not bothered with it the last two years, not since the death of his wife and daughter, but this year, this late morning, the loneliness and the monotony led him to it. He decided quite suddenly, having kept fairly good record on the calendar, that tomorrow was Christmas Eve, and zombies be damned, the Christmas lights and decorations were going up.

He went into the garage to look for the lights. He could hear the zombies sniffing around outside the garage door. The door was down and locked tight, and on top of that, though the zombies could grab and bite you, they weren't terribly strong most of the time, so the door was secure. The windows inside were boarded over, the doors were locked, and double locked, and boarded. The back yard the dead owned, but the windows and doors were boarded really well there, so he was shut in tight and safe.

Prowling through the holiday ornaments, he found immediately the large plastic Santa, and three long strings of lights. They were the ones he had ripped down in anger about two years back.

He managed all of the strings of lights into his living room. He plugged the wires into the extension cord that was hooked up to the generator he had put in the kitchen, and discovered most of the lights were as dead as the proverbial dodo bird. Many were broken from when he had torn them down.

He sat for a moment, then went to the little refrigerator he had replaced the big one with—used less energy—and pulled a bottled coffee out, twisted off the cap, and walked over to the living room window.

Unlike the garage on the side of the house, or the back yard, he had fenced the front yard off with deeply buried iron bars to which he had attached chicken wire, overlapped with barb wire. The fence rose to a height of eight feet. The gate, also eight feet tall, was made of the same. He seldom used it. He mostly went out and back in through the garage. There was no fence there. When he went out, they were waiting.

More often than not, he was able to run over and crush a few before hitting the door device, closing the garage behind him. On the way back, he rammed a few more, and with the touch of a button, sealed himself inside. When they were thin in the yard, he used that time to stack the bodies in his pickup truck, haul them somewhere to dump. It kept the stink down that way. Also, the rotting flesh tended to attract the hungry dead. The less he made them feel at home, the better.

Today, looking through the gaps between the boards nailed over the window, he could see the zombies beyond the fence. They were pulling at the wire, but it was firm and they were weak. He had discovered, strangely, that as it grew darker, they grew stronger. Nothing spectacular, but enough he could notice it. They were definitely faster then. It was as if the day made them sluggish, and the night rejuvenated them; gave them a shot of energy, like maybe the moon was their mistress.

He noticed too, that though there were plenty of them, there were fewer every day. He knew why. He had seen the results, not only around town, but right outside his fence. From time to time they just fell apart.

It was plain old natural disintegration. As time rolled on, their dead and rotten bodies came apart. For some reason, not as fast as was normal, but still, they did indeed break down. Of course, if they bit someone, they would become zombies, fresher ones, but, after the last six months there were few if any people left in town, besides himself. He didn't know how it was outside of town, but he assumed the results were similar. The zombies now, from time to time, turned on one another, eating what flesh they could manage to bite off each other's rotten bones. Dogs, cats, snakes, anything they could get their hands on, had been devastated. It was a new world, and it sucked. And sometimes it chewed.

Back in the garage, Calvin gathered up the six, large, plastic snowmen and the Santa, and pulled them into the house. He plugged them in and happily discovered they lit right up. But the strings of lights were still a problem. He searched the garage, and only found three spare bulbs— green ones—and when he screwed them in, only one worked. If he put up those strings they would be patchy. It wasn't as if anyone but himself would care, but a job worth doing was a job worth doing right, as his dad always said.

He smiled.

3

Ella, his wife, would have said it wasn't about doing a job right, it was more about fulfilling his compulsions. She would laugh at him now. Back then a crooked picture on the wall would make him crazy. Now there was nothing neat about the house. It was a fortress. It was a mess. It was a place to stay, but it wasn't a home.

Two years ago it ended being a home when he shot his wife and daughter in the head with the twelve gauge, put their bodies in the dumpster down the street, poured gas on them, and set them on fire.

All atmosphere of home was gone. Now, with him being the most desirable snack in town, just going outside the fence was a dangerous endeavor. And being inside he was as lonely as the guest of honor at a firing squad.

Calvin picked the strapped shotgun off the couch and flung it over his shoulder, adjusted the .38 revolver in his belt, grabbed the old fashioned tire tool from where it leaned in the corner, and went back to the garage.

He cranked up the truck, which he always backed in, and using the automatic garage opener, pressed it.

He had worked hard on the mechanism so that it would rise quickly and smoothly, and today was no exception. It yawned wide like a mouth opening. Three zombies, one he recognized faintly as Marilyn Paulson, a girl he had dated in high school, were standing outside. She had been his first love, his first sexual partner, and now half of her face dangled like a wash cloth on a clothes line. Her hair was falling out, and her eyes were set far back in her head, like dark marbles in crawfish holes.

The two others were men. One was reasonably fresh, but Calvin didn't recognize him. The other was his next door neighbor, Phil Tooney. Phil looked close to falling apart. Already his face had collapsed, his nose was gone, as well as both ears.

As Calvin roared the big four-seater pickup out of the garage, he hit Marilyn with the bumper and she went under, the wing mirror clipped Phil and sent him winding. He glanced in the rearview as he hit the garage mechanism, was pleased to see the door go down before the standing zombie could get inside. From time to time they got in when he left or returned, and he had to seal them in, get out and fight or shoot them. It was a major annoyance, knowing you had that waiting for you when you got back from town.

The last thing he saw as he drove away was the remaining zombie eating a mashed Marilyn as she squirmed on the driveway. He had shattered her legs with the truck. She was unable to fight back. The way his teeth clamped into her and pulled, it was as if he were trying to bite old bubble gum loose from the side walk.

Another glance in the mirror showed him Phil was back on his feet. He and the other zombie got into it then, fighting over the writhing meal on the cement. And then Calvin turned the truck along Seal Street, out of their view, and rolled on toward town.

Driving, he glanced at all the Christmas decorations. The lights strung on houses, no longer lit. The yard decorations, most of them knocked over: Baby Jesus flung south from an overturned manager, a deflated blow-up Santa Claus in a sleigh with hooked up reindeer, now lying like a puddle of lumpy paint spills in the high grass of a yard fronting a house with an open door.

As he drove, Calvin glanced at the dumpster by the side of the road. The one where he had put the bodies of his wife and daughter and burned them. It was, as far as he was concerned, their tomb.

One morning, driving into town for supplies, a morning like this, he had seen zombies in the dumpster, chewing at bones, strings of flesh. It had driven him crazy. He had pulled over right then and there and shotgunned them, blowing off two heads, and crushing in two others with the butt of the twelve gauge. Then, he had pulled the tire tool from his belt and beat their corpses to pieces. It had been easy, as they were rotten and ragged and almost gone. It was the brain being destroyed that stopped them, either that or their own timely disintegration, which with the destruction of the brain caused the rot to accelerate. But even with them down for the count, he kept whacking at them, screaming and crying as he did.

He swallowed as he drove by. Had he not been napping after a hard day's work, waiting on dinner, then he too would have been like Ella and Tina. He wasn't sure which was worse, becoming one of them, not knowing anything or anyone anymore, being eternally hungry, or surviving, losing his wife and daughter and having to remember them every day.

Mud Creek's Super Savor parking lot was full of cars and bones and wind blown shopping carts. A few zombies were wandering about. Somewhere gnawing the bones of the dead. A little child was down on her knees in the center of the lot gnawing on the head of a kitten.

As he drove up close to the Super Savor's side door, he got out quickly, with his key ready, the truck locked, the shotgun on his shoulder, and the tire tool in his belt.

He had, days after it all came down, finished off the walking dead in the Super Savor with his shotgun, and pulled their bodies out for the ones outside to feast on. While this went on, he found the electronic lock for the sliding plasti-glass doors, and he located the common doors at side and back, and found their keys. With the store sealed, he knew he could come in the smaller doors whenever he wanted, shop for canned and dried goods. The electricity was still working then, but in time, he feared it might go out. So he decided the best way to go was to start with the meats and fresh vegetables. They lasted for about six weeks. And then, for whatever reason, the electricity died.

It may have been attrition of power, or a terrific storm, though not nearly as terrific as the one Ella and Tina had described. The one that had changed things. But something killed the electricity. He managed to get a lot of meat out before then, and he tossed a lot away to keep it from rotting in the store, making the place stink.

By then, he had a freezer and the smaller refrigerator both hooked to gas generators he had taken from the store. And by siphoning gas from cars, he had been able to keep it running. He also worked out a way to maintain electricity by supplanting the gas powered generators with car batteries that he wired up and used until they died. Then he got others, fresh ones from the car parts house. He didn't know how long that supply would last. Someday he feared he would be completely in the dark when night fell. So, he made a point of picking up candles each time he went to the store. He had hundreds of them now, big fat ones, and plenty of matches.

The weather was cool, so he decided on canned chili and crackers. There was plenty of food in the store, as most of the town had seen the storm and been affected by it, and had immediately gone into zombie mode. For them, it was no more cheese and crackers, salads with dressing on the side, now it was hot, fresh meat and cold dead meat, rotting on the bone.

As he cruised the aisle, he saw a rack with bags of jerky on it. He hadn't had jerky in ages. He grabbed bags of it and threw them in the cart. He found a twelve pack of bottled beer and put that in the cart.

He was there for about six hours. Just wandering. Thinking. He used the restrooms, which still flushed. He had the same luxury at his house, and he could have waited, but the whole trip, the food, walking the aisles, using the toilet, it was akin to a vacation.

After a while he went to the section of the store that contained the decorations. He filled another basket with strings of lights, and even located a medium sized plastic Christmas tree. Three baskets were eventually filled, one with the plastic tree precariously balanced on top. He found a Santa hat, said, "What the hell," and put it on.

He pushed all three baskets near the door he had come in. He slung the shotgun off his shoulder, and took a deep breath. He hated this part. You never knew what was behind the door. The automatic doors would have been better in this regard, as they were hard plastic and you could see through them, but the problem was if you went out that way, you left the automatic door working, and they could come and go inside as they pleased. He liked the store to be his sanctuary, just like the pawn shop downtown, the huge car parts store, and a number of other places he had rigged with locks and hidden weapons.

He stuck the key in the door and heard it snick. He opened it quickly. They weren't right at the door, but they were all around his truck. He got behind one of the baskets and pushed it out, leaving the door behind him open. It was chancy, as one of them might slip inside unseen, even be waiting a week or two later when he came back, but it was a chance he had to take.

Pushing the basket hard, he rushed out into the lot and to the back of the truck. He had to pause to open up with the shotgun. He dropped four of them, then realized he was out of fire power. For the first time in ages, he had forgot to check the loads in the gun; his last trek out, a trip to the pawn shop, had used most of them, and he hadn't reloaded.

He couldn't believe it. He was slipping. And you couldn't slip. Not in this world.

He pulled the .38 revolver and popped off a shot, missed. Two were closing. He stuck the revolver back in his belt, grabbed a handful of goodies from the basket and tossed them in the back of the pickup. When he looked up, four were closing, and down the way, stumbling over the parking lot, were more of them. A lot of them. In that moment, all he could think was: at least they're slow.

He pulled the .38 again, but one of them came out of nowhere, grabbed him by the throat. He whacked at the arm with revolver, snapped it off at the shoulder, leaving the hand still gripping him. The zombie, minus an arm, lunged toward him, snapping its teeth, filling the air with its foul stench.

At close range he didn't miss with the revolver, got Armless right between the eyes. He jerked the arm free of his neck, moved forward quickly, and using the pistol as a club, which for him was more precise, he knocked two down, crushing one's skull, and finishing off the other with a close skull shot. A careful shot dropped another.

He looked to see how fast the other zombies were coming. Not that fast. They were just halfway across the lot.

There was one more zombie near the front of his truck. It had circled the vehicle while he was fighting the others. He hadn't even seen where it came from. He watched it as he finished unloading the car. When it was close, he shot it at near point blank range, causing its rotten skull to explode like a pumpkin, spewing what appeared to be boiled, dirty oatmeal all over the side of his truck and the parking lot.

Darting back inside, he managed to push one cart out, and then shove the other after it. He grabbed the handles of the carts, one in each hand, and guided them to the back of the truck. The zombies were near now. One of them, for some reason, was holding his hand high above his head, as if in greeting. Calvin was tempted to wave.

Calvin tossed everything in the back of the truck and was dismayed to hear a bulb or two from his string of bulbs pop. The last thing he tossed in back was the Christmas tree.

He was behind the wheel and backing around even before the zombies arrived. He drove toward them, hit two and crunched them down.

As if it mattered, as he wheeled out of the lot, he tossed up his hand in a one finger salute.

"They were so pretty," Ella had said about the lightning flashes. She had awakened him as he lay snoozing on the couch.

"They were red and yellow and green and blue and all kinds of colors," Tina said. "Come on, daddy, come see."

By the time he was there, the strange lightning storm was gone. There was only the rain. It had come out of nowhere, caused by who knew what. Even the rain came and went quickly; a storm that covered the earth briefly, flashed lights, spit rain, and departed.

When the rain stopped, the people who had observed the colored lightning died, just keeled over. Ella and Tina among them, dropped over right in the living room on Christmas Eve, just before presents were to be opened.

It made no sense. But that's what happened. Then, even as he tried to revive them, they rose.

Immediately, he knew they weren't right. It didn't take a wizard to realize that. They came at him, snarling, long strings of mucus flipping from their mouths like rabid dog saliva. They tried to bite him. He pushed them back, he called their names, he yelled, he pleaded, but still they came, biting and snapping. He stuck a couch cushion in Ella's mouth.

She grabbed it and ripped it. Stuffing flew like a snow storm. And he ran.

He hid in the bedroom, locked the door, not wanting to hurt them. He heard the others, his neighbors, outside, roaming around the house. He looked out the window. There were people all over the back yard, fighting with one another, some of them living, trying to survive, going down beneath teeth and nails. People like him, who for some reason had not seen the weird storm. But the rest were dead. Like his wife and daughter. The lights of the storm had stuck something behind their eyes that killed them and brought them back—dead, but walking, and hungry.

Ella and Tina pounded on his bedroom door with the intensity of a drum solo. Bam, bam, bam, bam, bam, bam. He sat on the bed for an hour, his hands over his ears, tears streaming down his face, listening to his family banging at the door, hearing the world outside coming apart.

He took a deep breath, got the shotgun out of the closet, made sure it was loaded, opened the bedroom door.

It was funny, but he could still remember thinking as they went through the doorway, *Here's my gift to you. Merry Christmas, family. I love you.*

And then two shots.

Later, when things had settled, he had managed, even in the midst of a zombie takeover, to take their bodies to the dumpster, pour gas on them, and dispose of them as best he could. Months later, from

13

time to time, he would awaken, the smell of their burning flesh and the odor of gasoline in his nostrils.

Later, one post at a time, fighting off zombies as he worked, he built his compound to keep them out, to give him a yard, a bit of normalcy.

Calvin looked in the rear view mirror. His forehead was beaded with sweat. He was still wearing the Santa hat. The snowball on its tip had fallen onto the side of his face. He flipped it back, kept driving.

He was almost home when he saw the dog and saw them chasing it. The dog was skinny, near starved, black and white spotted, probably some kind of hound mix. It was running all out, and as it was nearing dark, the pace of the zombies had picked up. By deep night fall, they would be able to move much faster. That dog was dead meat.

The dog cut out into the road in front of him, and he braked. Of the four zombies chasing the dog, only one of them stopped to look at him. The other three ran on.

Calvin said, "Eat bumper," gassed the truck into the zombie who had stopped to stare, knocking it under the pickup. He could hear it dragging underneath as he drove. The other zombies were chasing the dog down the street, gaining on it; it ran with its tongue hanging long.

The dog swerved off the road and jetted between houses. The zombies ran after it. Calvin started to let it go. It wasn't his problem. But, as if without thought, he wheeled the truck off the road and across a yard. He caught one of the zombies, a fat slow one that had most likely been fat and slow in life. He bounced the truck over it and bore down on the other two.

One heard the motor, turned to look, and was scooped under the bumper so fast it looked like a magic act disappearance. The other didn't seem to notice him at all. It was so intent on its canine lunch. Calvin hit it with the truck, knocked it against the side of a house, pinned it there, gassed the truck until it snapped in two and the house warped under the pressure.

Calvin backed off, fearing he might have damaged the engine. But the truck still ran.

He looked. The dog was standing between two houses, panting, its pink tongue hanging out of its mouth like a bright power tie.

Opening the door, Calvin called to the dog. The dog didn't move, but its ears sprang up.

"Come on, boy...girl. Come on, doggie." The dog didn't move.

Calvin looked over his shoulders. Zombies were starting to appear everywhere. They were far enough away he could make an escape, but close enough to be concerned.

And then he saw the plastic Christmas tree had been knocked out of the back of the pickup. He ran over and picked it up and tossed it in the bed. He looked at the dog.

"It's now are never, pup," Calvin said. "Come on. I'm not one of them."

It appeared the dog understood completely. It came toward him, tail wagging. Calvin bent down, carefully extended his hand toward it. He patted it on the head. Its tail went crazy. The dog had a collar on. There was a little aluminum tag in the shape of a bone around its neck. He took it between thumb and forefinger. The dog's name was stenciled on it: BUFFY. Looking back at the zombies coming across the yard in near formation,

Calvin spoke to the dog, "Come on, Buffy. Go with me."

He stepped back, one hand on the open door. The dog sprang past him, into the seat. Calvin climbed in, backed around, and they were out of there, slamming zombies right and left as the truck broke their lines.

As he neared his house, the sun was starting to dip. The sky was as purple as a hammered plum. Behind him, in the mirror, he could see zombies coming from all over, between houses, out of houses, down the road, moving swiftly.

He gave the truck gas, and then a tire blew.

The truck's rear end skidded hard left, almost spun, but Calvin fought the wheel and righted it. It bumped along, and he was forced to slow it down to what seemed like a near crawl. In the rear view, he could see the dead gaining; a sea of teeth and putrid faces. He glanced at the dog. It was staring out the back window as well, a look of concern on its face.

"I shouldn't have stopped for you," Calvin said, and in an instant he thought, *If I opened the door and kicked you out, that might slow them down. They might stop and fight over a hot lunch.*

It was a fleeting thought.

"You go, I go," Calvin said, as if he had owned the dog for years, as if it were a part of his family.

He kept driving, bumping the pickup along.

When he arrived at his house, he didn't have time to back in as usual. He hit the garage remote and drove the truck inside. When he got out, Buffy clamoring out behind him, the zombies were in the garage, maybe ten of them, others in the near distance were moving faster and faster toward him.

Calvin touched the remote, closed the garage door, trapping himself and the dog inside with those ten, but keeping the others out. He tossed the remote on the hood of the pickup, pulled the pistol and used what ammunition was left. A few of them were hit in the head and dropped. He jammed the empty pistol in his belt, pulled the tire iron free, began to swing it, cracking heads with the blows.

He heard growling and ripping, turned to see Buffy had taken one down and was tearing its throat out, pulling its near rotten head off its shoulders.

"Good dog, Buffy," Calvin yelled, and swung the iron. "Sic 'em."

They came over the roof of the truck. One of them, a woman, leaped on him and knocked him face down, sent his tire iron flying. She went rolling into the wall, but was up quickly and moving toward him.

He knew this was it. He sensed another close on him, and then another, and then he heard the dog bark, growl. Calvin managed to turn his head slightly as Buffy leaped and hit the one above him, knocking her down. It wasn't much, but it allowed Calvin to scramble to his feet, start swinging the tire iron. Left and right he swung it, with all his might.

They came for him, closer. He backed up, Buffy beside him, their asses against the wall, the zombies in front of them. There were three of the dead left. They came like bullets. Calvin breathed hard. He grabbed the tire iron off the garage floor, swung it as quickly and as firmly as he could manage, dodging in between them, not making a kill shot, just knocking them aside, finally dashing for the truck with Buffy at his heels. Calvin and Buffy jumped inside, and Calvin slammed the door and locked it. The zombies slammed against the door and the window, but it held.

Calvin got a box of .38 shells out of the glove box, pulled the revolver from his belt and loaded it. He took a deep breath. He looked out the driver's side window where one of the zombies, maybe male, maybe female, too far gone to tell, tried to chew the glass.

When he had driven inside, he had inadvertently killed the engine. He reached and twisted the key, started it up.

Then he pushed back against Buffy, until they were as close to the other door as possible. Then he used his toe to roll down the glass where the zombie gnashed. As the window dropped, its head dipped inward and its teeth snapped at the air. The revolver barked, knocking a hole in the zombie's head, spurting a gusher of goo, causing it to spin and drop as if practicing a ballet move.

Another showed its face at the open window, and got the same reception.

A .38 slug.

Calvin twisted in his seat and looked at the other window. Nothing. Where was the last one? He eased to the middle, pulling the dog beside him. As he held the dog, he could feel it shivering. Damn, what a dog. Terrified, and still a fighter. No quitter was she.

A hand darted through the open window, tried to grab him, snatched off his Santa hat. He spun around to shoot. The zombie arm struck the pistol, sent it flying. It grabbed him. It had him now, and this one, fresher than the others, was strong. It pulled him toward the window, toward snapping, jagged teeth.

Buffy leaped. It was a tight fit between Calvin and the window, but the starved dog made it, hit the zombie full in the face and slammed it backwards. Buffy fell out the window after it.

Calvin found the pistol, jumped out of the car. The creature had grabbed Buffy by the throat, had spun her around on her back, and was hastily dropping its head for the bite.

Calvin fired. The gun took off the top of the thing's head. It let go of Buffy. It stood up, stared at him, made two quick steps toward him, and dropped. The dog charged to Calvin's side, growling.

"It's all right, girl. It's all right. You done good. Damn, you done good."

Calvin got the tire iron and went around and carefully bashed in all the heads of the zombies, just for insurance. Tomorrow, he'd change the tire on the truck, probably blown out from running over zombies. He'd put his spare on it, the donut tire, drive to the tire store and find four brand new ones and put them on. Tomorrow he'd get rid of the zombie's bodies. Tomorrow he'd do a lot of things.

But not tonight.

He found the Santa hat and put it back on. Tonight, he had other plans.

First he gave Buffy a package of jerky. She ate like the starving animal she was. He got a bowl out of the shelf and filled it with water.

"From now on, that's your bowl, girl. Tomorrow... maybe the next day, I'll find you some canned dog food at the store."

He got another bowl and opened a can of chili

and poured it into the bowl. He was most likely over-feeding her. She'd probably throw it up. But that was all right. He would clean it up, and tomorrow they'd start over, more carefully. But tonight, Buffy had earned a special treat.

He went out and got the tree out of the truck and put it up and put ornaments on it from two years back. Ornaments he had left on the floor after throwing the old dead and dried tree over the fence. This plastic one was smaller, but it would last, year after year.

He sat down under the tree and found the presents he had for his wife and child. He pushed them aside, leaving them wrapped. He opened those they had given him two Christmases ago. He liked all of them. The socks. The underwear. The ties he would never wear. DVDs of movies he loved, and would watch, sitting on the couch with Buffy, who he would soon make fat.

He sat for a long time and looked at his presents and cried.

Using the porch light for illumination, inside the fenced-in yard, he set about putting up the decorations. Outside the fence the zombies grabbed at it, and rattled it, and tugged, but it held. It was a good fence. A damn good fence. He believed in that te-diously built fence. And the zombies weren't good climbers. They got off the ground, it was like some of whatever made them animated slid out of them in invisible floods. It was as if they gained their living dead status from the earth itself.

It was a long job, and when he finished climbing the ladder, stapling up the lights, making sure the Santa and snow men were in their places, he went inside and plugged it all in.

When he came outside, the yard was lit in colors of red and blue and green. The Santa and the snowmen glowed as if they had swallowed lightning.

Buffy stood beside him, wagging her tail as they examined the handiwork.

Then Calvin realized something. It had grown very quiet. The fence was no longer being shaken or pulled. He turned quickly toward where the zombies stood outside the fence. They weren't holding onto the wire anymore. They weren't moaning. They weren't doing anything except looking, heads lifted toward the lights.

Out there in the shadows, the lights barely touching them with a fringe of color, they looked like happy and surprised children.

"They like it," Calvin said, and looked down at Buffy. She looked up at him, wagging her tail.

"Merry Christmas, dog."

When he glanced up, he saw a strange thing. One of the zombies, a woman, a barefoot woman wearing shorts and a tee-shirt, a young woman, maybe even a nice looking woman not so long ago, lifted her arm and pointed at the lights and smiled with dark, rotting teeth. Then there came a sound from all of them, like a contented sigh.

"I'll be damned," Calvin said. "They like it."

He thought: I will win. I will wait them out. They will all fall apart someday soon. But tonight, they are here with us, to share the lights. They are our company. He got a beer from inside, came back out and pulled up a lawn chair and sat down. Buffy lay down beside him. He was tempted to give those poor sonofabitches outside the wire a few strips of jerky. Instead, he sipped his beer.

A tear ran down his face as he yelled toward the dead. "Merry Christmas, you monsters. Merry Christmas to all of you, and to all a good night."

CHRISTMAS with the DEAD

Screenplay by

Keith Lansdale

CHRISTMAS WITH THE DEAD

Written by
Keith Lansdale

Adapted from the short story by
Joe R. Lansdale

CHRISTMAS MUSIC PLAYING over
blackness.

INT. RADIO STATION - HALLWAY - DAY

LOW TO THE GROUND, RAY wearing muddy,
torn pants only seen from the waist
down, slowly shuffling toward us in
zombie-like fashion, dragging one leg
behind the other as he makes his way
down the hall.
He gets to a door at the end of the
hall and-

CLOSE ON a dirty fist, clumsily slamming against the door. Not knocking on
it as much as knocking against it.

BLAM BLAM

RADIO STATION - DJ BOOTH - DAY - CON-
TINUOUS

Shot of the same door from the other
side surrounded by the lights and
gizmos running the station.

BLAM BLAM

RADIO STATION - DJ BOOTH DOORWAY - DAY
- CONTINUOUS

The door is snatched open, and we see RAY's face. A little bloody, a lot of muddy. He has a vacant expression, like a look of the undead.

>   CALVIN (O.S.)
>   Good lord, Ray. You look dead.

We see RAY IN FULL. He's carrying a small cardboard box tucked under one arm, mud splotches from head to toe.

>   RAY
>   Some old lady pushed me down.

RADIO STATION - DJ BOOTH - DAY - CONTINUOUS

Deeper into the room we see a chair next to a microphone and switchboard, lights blinking on the many machines and computers inside. It looks like Christmas.

CALVIN, a man in his mid 20s, is holding the door open for Ray who's limping inside with the box.

>   CALVIN
>   What happened to your leg?

                    RAY
    I think I twisted my ankle or
        something when I fell.

The CHRISTMAS MUSIC starts to wind
down and Calvin takes the seat in
front of the music console.

                  CALVIN
          Hold that thought…

The song comes to an end and Calvin
looks up at a lady through a large
glass window who gives him a thumbs up
as the ON AIR sign lights up.

Calvin's in the zone.

              CALVIN (CONT'D)
        That was the latest tune from
        Kasey Lansdale, bringing the
        holiday cheer to our little
        station today. Speaking of
    bringing cheer to the station, we
      just got our latest collection
       for the food drive and it looks
              like we got…

Calvin motions to Ray to let him look
in the box.

Ray steps forward and Calvin peers inside, fishing around inside.

> CALVIN (CONT'D)
> Well, looks like we got some
> canned corn and…

Calvin pulls out a can of tuna.

> CALVIN (CONT'D)
> Several more cans of tuna. Well,
> I'm not a huge fan, but I know the
> effort is appreciated. Remember,
> even though it's Christmas Eve,
> you still have time to make those
> donations for the people who need
> them. Just drop them off at one of
> the spots we've been talking about
> all month or bring them down to
> the station. We're next to Pippo's
> Used Cars on Barrett Street.

Calvin hits a couple switches and AN-
OTHER CHRISTMAS SONG starts back up as
Calvin signs off over the music with-

> CALVIN (CONT'D)
> That's going to be all for me
> tonight. I'm signing off for the
> night to catch the next one-horse

sleigh home with plans to deck my
halls and hope for a silent
night. Merry Christmas Eve
everyone, and keep it tuned to
K.Z.O.M. radio.

Calvin flips another switch, and he's
out. The ON AIR light goes dark as the
Christmas music plays on.

He turns back to Ray.

> CALVIN (CONT'D)
> More tuna?

> RAY
> At least people are giving.

> CALVIN
> I guess.

> RAY
> Calvin, is it alright if I leave
> too? Wanted to be home before
> Kara so I can have dinner ready
> and get my Christmas outfit on.

> CALVIN
> Might as well. Place pretty much
> runs itself tonight.

31

RAY

You guys want to come over? We
got plenty of food and you guys
could just walk over when you're
ready.

CALVIN

No, no. Wouldn't want to impose.

RAY

If you change your mind…

Calvin stands up and takes the box
from Ray over to a corner with other
boxes like it.

CALVIN

An old woman beat you up?

RAY

I got between her and the last
eggnog. Next thing I know, I
can't put any weight on this leg.

CALVIN

There was mud near the eggnog?

RAY

I fell in the mud after…

Calvin looks at Ray.

RAY (CONT'D)
...Cause of the leg.

CALVIN
(sarcastically)
Christmas really brings out the
best in people.

EXT. DOWN RANDOM STREETS - EVENING -
LATER

We glide down different streets as we
see Christmas lights being turned on
as the sun sets.

TITLE: *Christmas With The Dead*

The opening credits roll as we see
more and more lights come on. Motorized decorations moving in yards. Kids
in windows shaking presents which were
pulled from beneath Christmas trees.

We pull into the sky and see all the
houses below, glowing with Christmas
cheer, but we aren't stopping.

Higher through the clouds. We're still
pulling back out of the atmosphere of
Earth. Passing a blinking satellite as
we pass through the exosphere and then

into the nothingness of space - and we
see - the lightning.

They quietly ZAP and bounce around,
electrifying the area around it. A
ball of colored energy headed right
toward Earth.

The ball of lightning hits the satellite, quietly tearing it to bits. On-
ward it goes, leaving the satellite
dead, the blinking lights like burnt
out Christmas bulbs.

EXT. CALVIN'S NEIGHBORHOOD - EVENING -
LATER

Calvin's neighborhood is down a cul-
de-sac, with Calvin's house straight
up the middle. All the houses have a
few Christmas decorations.

Nothing extravagant, but it's certainly Christmas. All except Calvin's
which is plain and undecorated.

The houses on either side of him are
Ray's and FRANK's. In front of Frank's
house in the driveway is a nice,
older-model convertible, one that
screams mid-life crises.

A middle-aged man, FRANK, in shorts, a ponytail, and shades pushed back on the top of his head, is using a rag to wipe the car down.

Calvin's truck, an older model with dents and a worn look, pulls up to the end of Frank's drive.

Calvin rolls down the window.

> CALVIN
> That thing's a beaut, Frank.

Frank walks over to Calvin's truck.

> FRANK
> Worth every penny.

> CALVIN
> I wish I had enough pennies.

> FRANK
> Maybe one day.

> CALVIN
> Just hope it's before the world
> ends.

Frank leans in the window.

                    FRANK
        I'm sure you do pretty well
        between you and the misses.

                    CALVIN
             We do all right.

Calvin pauses.

                CALVIN (CONT'D)
        Truthfully, no one listens to the
        radio these days. Hopefully I'll
        still have a job this time next
                    year.

                    FRANK
             (not really listening)
        Yeah, it's tough all over.

                    CALVIN
               That it is.

They both sit there a moment. Frank
taps his finger against the truck.

                CALVIN (CONT'D)
        Everything going good with you?

                    FRANK
        Nothing special honestly.

Frank thinks a second.

                    FRANK (CONT'D)
          Oh! Did you hear about the guy
             that sold me the car?

                    CALVIN
          Just what you told me.

                    FRANK
          Guy got arrested.

                    CALVIN
          What?

                    FRANK
          Yeah. Few months ago. Probably
          not long after I bought the car
             from him, really.

                    CALVIN
          No shit?

                    FRANK
          No shit. Right there on the car
          lot. The one near your station.

                    CALVIN
          What'd he do?

                    FRANK

I'm not completely sure, but I
heard he was part of some
religious cult trying to
sacrifice people who they didn't
believe were
(uses finger quotes)
"holy" enough.

CALVIN
Wow.

FRANK
Nuts, right? Guy seemed normal.

CALVIN
They usually do.

Frank shrugs.

FRANK
Either way, I'm just glad he got
me a good deal before they
got him.

CALVIN
That's what really matters.

Frank laughs.

CALVIN (CONT'D)

> All right, well I better get
> home.

                    FRANK
> You going to put some lights up?
> It is Christmas Eve. Calvin looks
> up at his bare home.

INSERT: CALVIN'S HOME, not a single
decoration.

                    FRANK (CONT'D)
> Even Ray put his lights up.
> You're the only bare spot in the
> neighborhood.

BACK TO SCENE

Calvin looks at Ray's house. The house
on the other side of his.

                    CALVIN
> You sound like Ella.

                    FRANK
> 'Tis the season.

                    CALVIN
> So I've heard.

                                      39

INT. CALVIN'S HOUSE - GARAGE - EVENING
- CONTINUOUS

Every corner has a pile of boxes. Some
look organized, some just thrown on
top of each other.

The garage door is still open behind
him, letting light inside.

Calvin gets out of his truck and
starts toward the door that would lead
inside the house.

He stops and walks over to one of the
piles of boxes and peers inside, not
finding what he's looking for. He
pushes it aside, looks inside another
box. More of the same.

He spies a nearby pile and looks inside. Jackpot. He pulls out a wad of
Christmas lights, knotted to hell.

He surveys the mess of lights and
spots a plug twisted in it, pulling it
away from the pile just enough.

He walks over to an outlet and plugs
it in.
Nothing.

Unplugs. Plugs it back in again. Still nothing.

He dumps the whole ball into a large trash can and heads for the door again hitting a switch nearby closing the RUMBLING garage door as he heads into-

INT. CALVIN'S HOUSE - KITCHEN -
EVENING - CONTINUOUS

                    TINA
                  Daddy!

TINA, a young girl about 8, runs up to Calvin as he stoops down to greet her. She's holding Mr. Bear, a stuffed teddy bear, lovingly but closer to having it in a headlock.

                   CALVIN
                Little One!

Calvin picks her up and holds her as she's holding the bear. Doing the best he can to shut the door and come inside now with his arms full.

                    TINA
        Daddy, Mommy said Santa got my
                   letter!

41

                    CALVIN
        I'm sure he did. What did you ask
        Santa for? Nothing too expensive
                    I hope.

                    TINA
        Santa's magic silly. He doesn't
                have money.

                    CALVIN
            You're right. Silly me.

ELLA, Calvin's wife, has been standing
there watching.

Calvin notices Ella and sets Tina down
as she drops Mr. Bear and runs off to
the other room.

Calvin reaches down and picks up Mr.
Bear.

                CALVIN (CONT'D)
                  (to Ella)
        Did we…Santa get all his shopping
                    done?

                    ELLA
                  (feisty)
            Santa did his job. See, I can
                count on Santa.

42

                    CALVIN
          Meaning…what? That you can't
                count on me?

                     ELLA
              Apparently not.

                    CALVIN
          Is this about the lights?

                     ELLA
          Every year it's the same thing.
                    (mocking)
          Baby, I'm going to get them right
               after work, I promise.
                    (normal)
             Then every year, you throw
          together a half-ass attempt, if
              you even do that much.

                    CALVIN
                     Baby…

                     ELLA
                 (sarcastically)
                   Here we go…

          Calvin doesn't say anything.

                 ELLA (CONT'D)
          I just want Tina to enjoy the

                                        43

           magic of Christmas a little
                    longer.

                    CALVIN
                   (laughing)
            "The magic of Christmas."

Ella shooting daggers out of her
eyes.

                 CALVIN (CONT'D)
             I'm just tired after working
                   all day.

                     ELLA
        I work all day, too, and I get my
                 things done.

Calvin starts to say something, but
stops. He knows she's right.

He's looking for a way to diffuse the
tension.

He raises Mr. Bear in front of his
face and makes it look like Mr. Bear
is talking, using a funny voice.

                    CALVIN
                 (as Mr. Bear)
         Mr. Bear and I are vewy sowwy.

                    ELLA
        You're not going to get out of
         this by doing the damn bear
                    voice.

                   CALVIN
                (as Mr. Bear)
            But I'm going to twy.

Ella tries to stay angry, but it's a
losing battle.

              CALVIN (CONT'D)
                (as Mr. Bear)
        Mommy was wight. Daddy is going
        to go to the store and see what
            decorations he can find.

Calvin peeks from behind the bear at
Ella who's trying to hide a smile.

                    ELLA
             (trying to stay angry)
        There'd be more at the store if
            you didn't wait last minute.

Calvin makes an exaggerated sad face,
holding Mr. Bear close by.
Ella lets out a tiny laugh.

                   CALVIN

                    (in his normal voice)
                Theeeere she is.

Calvin steps forward and hugs Ella who
hesitates, and then hugs him back.

                    ELLA
        You better be glad I love you so
                    much.

                    CALVIN
                    I am.

They kiss.

INT. CALVIN'S HOUSE - LIVING ROOM -
NIGHT - LATER

A Christmas tree done up nice. It's a
fake tree, with lights and ornaments
and several presents tucked under.
It's against a large window, the cur-
tains pulled back shining out to the
whole neighborhood.

There's a string of Christmas lights
around the window.

Nearby is a couch with a Christmas-
theme quilt thrown across the back.

Ella and Tina are putting more ornaments on the tree.

Ella is dressed cute like Mrs. Claus
and Tina is dressed like an elf. It's
just all part of the fun.

Tina is holding an ornament, about to
hang it when bright lights of every
color flash in the window.

                    TINA
     Santa's here! Santa's here!

Tina runs over to the window to look
out, Ella a few steps behind her.

                    ELLA
     It's a little early for Santa…

They both look out.

EXT. CALVIN'S YARD - NIGHT - CON-
TINUOUS

Bright lights explode overhead. It
looks like lightening, except for all
the different colors tearing across
the night sky.

Tina and Ella looking out the window, peering into the sky.

> **TINA**
> It's Santa! It's Santa!

Ella opens the window and leans her head out looking into the night sky.

INT. CALVIN'S HOUSE - GARAGE - NIGHT - CONTINUOUS

Calvin's sitting in the middle of the pile of boxes where he found the lights, digging around in them. Random crap strewn around from boxes he's already searched.

A couple old looking Christmas decorations set nearby, all in need of being replaced.

He pulls out some long candy canes decorations for the walkway.

> **ELLA (O.S.)**
> Calvin! Come look at these lights!

> **CALVIN**
> (shouting back to Ella)

I think I found some of the older
stuff. Not sure how much of it's
any good.

Calvin waits for a response.

> CALVIN (CONT'D)
> Ella?

Calvin's face turns serious.

> CALVIN (CONT'D)
> Ella?

INT. CALVIN'S HOUSE - LIVING ROOM -
NIGHT - CONTINUOUS

Ella and Tina are both laying next to
the tree. A beautiful tree next to a
horrible sight.

Both Ella and Tina are still.

Both not breathing.

Calvin rushes over to Tina and Ella,
trying to stir them.

> CALVIN
> (panicky)
> Little one? Tina?

He looks to Ella who's the same.

> CALVIN (CONT'D)
> Ella? Ella!?

Still nothing.

INT. CALVIN'S HOUSE - KITCHEN - NIGHT
- CONTINUOUS

Calvin standing in the doorway between
the kitchen and living room, snatching
a landline phone hanging from the
wall.
We can see the living room through the
doorway, a direct view of Tina.

INSERT PHONE: dialing 911 with audible
BEEPS as he dials.

BACK TO CALVIN who's listening to the
receiver-

Nothing.

BACKGROUND: Tina silently sits up,
then staggers to her feet.

Calvin doesn't notice, too frantic
again dialing the phone.

CHRISTMAS WITH THE DEAD

Tina wanders to the open window, leans
into it and tumbles out.

Calvin dials again and listens. But
again, nothing.

                CALVIN
          Work, God damn it!

Calvin continues to dial the phone
with little luck.

Calvin slams the phone down frustrated
and heads for the front yard.

EXT. CALVIN'S YARD - NIGHT - CON-
TINUOUS

Calvin comes out in a panic.

                CALVIN
             (to anyone)
        Help! Help! I need help!

He looks across the cul-de-sac to see
a lifeless world decorated for
Christmas.

A CAR ALARM BLARES somewhere out of
sight.

51

He's looking into the distance when a familiar face appears.

Ray, and he's in a panic. Wearing a shirt covered in presents and a giant hat shaped like a Christmas tree.

He's holding a bloody hammer in one hand and still walking with a limp.

                    RAY
    Calvin! I need to use your phone!

                    CALVIN
                (in a daze)
        Phone's not working, Ray.

Ray never slows, heading right into the house.

INT. CALVIN'S HOUSE - KITCHEN - NIGHT - CONTINUOUS

Ray's dialing the phone, much like Calvin was.

Calvin has followed Ray back inside, moving on auto pilot.

                    RAY
    My cell's not working. You're the

only one I know who still has a
home phone.

                    CALVIN
                  (stunned)
It's not working, Ray. I already
                   tried.

                     RAY
We need an ambulance, Calvin.
Something terrible happened.

                    CALVIN
            I know Ray, it's…

                     RAY
        No, Calvin. You don't…

Ray holds up the hammer, visible blood
is on it.

Calvin looks at Ray for answers.

Ray hesitates. He doesn't want
to say.

                 RAY (CONT'D)
                  …Tina.

                    CALVIN
                   What?

                    RAY
          I think I hurt Tina.

                  CALVIN
       Hurt Tina? What are you saying?

                    RAY
       I found a few more lights I was
              about to hang up...
          (he motions with the hammer)
        And Tina ran inside and bit me.

                  CALVIN
                 Bit you?

Calvin looks confused.

Ray shows Calvin bloody teeth marks on
his leg.

                    RAY
          Same leg from before.

Calvin grabs Ray's shoulders, lightly
shaking him as he talks.

                  CALVIN
       Are you fucking with me? What's
       wrong with you? Tina didn't bite
         anyone. She just collapsed. I
              tried to call 911...

                    RAY
          (looking at the bloody hammer)
          Calvin. She surprised me. I hit
            her. Oh God, I hit her so
                      hard.

Ray looking shocked, no longer taking
in the world around him.

Calvin lets go and heads into-

INT. CALVIN'S HOUSE - LIVING ROOM -
NIGHT - CONTINUOUS

Not only is there no Tina, but Ella is
standing at the window, looking out as
if taking in the night air.

                    CALVIN
                 (surprised)
                   Ella!

He starts to rush over to her.

Ella hears Calvin and turns around
slowly, but she's no longer Ella.
She's off center, leaning oddly.

ELLA CLOSE UP: colored lights zap
across her eyes as they make a noise
like an ELECTRIC ZAP!

Calvin can tell she's not right. He
stops in his tracks.

> CALVIN (CONT'D)
> Ella?

Calvin slowly steps closer as the
gears in Ella's head turn, processing
a thought. Is it recognition?

It's HUNGER! Ella lunges at Calvin
like a starved dog spotting a rabbit.

Calvin catches her at the shoulders,
pinning her arms down, holding her
back as she snaps her teeth and her
eyes light up with ZAPS!

She's strong. Stronger than she
should be. She's closing the gap as
Calvin can't hold her back much
longer.

> CALVIN (CONT'D)
> Ray! Ray! Help!

Ray comes back in, wielding the hammer. Calvin spots him.

> CALVIN (CONT'D)
> Not the hammer, Ray! Grab her!

Ray grabs Ella and successfully pulls
her away. Only it's more bad news
for Ray.

Ella sinks her teeth into Ray's neck,
biting out a huge chunk of flesh and
pulling it free.

Ray pushes her away and stumbles back
until he hits the wall, then sliding
down the wall leaving a bloody streak,
still holding the hammer.

Ella turns again and rushes Calvin as
he snags the quilt from the couch and
throws it over Ella's head, then tackling her onto the couch, successfully
pinning her down. Except now he's
stuck holding her there.

Ray's not looking too good.

                    RAY
      Oh fuck. Now your whole family's
              bit me.

                  CALVIN
               Ray! Help!

                    RAY
               Fuck me!

Ray finds a bit of strength, and comes to Calvin holding up the hammer.

                    CALVIN
          Damn it, Ray. I said NOT the
          hammer! Something to tie her
                    down.

Ray looks around and spots the Christmas lights around the window. He grabs an end and yanks them free.

Calvin pulls Ella into a sitting position as Ray wraps the lights around her, successfully trapping her in the quilt.

Ray takes a seat next to the wiggling quilt, and a stunned Calvin.

He's moments from checking out.

                    RAY
          Worst. Christmas. Ever.

Ray goes quiet.

Calvin gets up, watching the quilt wiggle and Ray no longer move.

He HEARS a THUMPING from outside the window.

He shuts the window as the face of Frank appears, also zombiefied, blood around his mouth, looking at Calvin like he is a big Christmas turkey.

Calvin quickly shuts the curtain and turns away. If he can't see it, it can't be real.

EXT. CALVIN'S YARD - MORNING - SIX MONTHS LATER

The same house from before, a chain-link fence now surrounding the property line.

Calvin is standing outside wearing a robe over Christmas theme PJs, staring at the house.

He's holding a cup of coffee.

                    CALVIN
                 (to himself)
         I think I have it this time.

Calvin takes a sip of the coffee and

then makes a face as if someone shit
in his cup.

Calvin starts walking back inside the
house as he pours it out on the lawn.

INT. CALVIN'S HOUSE - BEDROOM - MO-
MENTS LATER

Calvin pokes his head in the door.

A CHAIN RATTLES, but we don't see what
it is.

                    CALVIN
        I think I have it figured.

Calvin walks in holding a pink dog
bowl with a fresh out of the can
cylinder of dog food still poking out
of it.

Again the CHAIN RATTLES.

Calvin leans down and sets the bowl on
the ground right over a line of duct
tape he's put on the floor, careful
not to cross it himself.

Calvin stands up. And we see her-

Ella. Six months of zombie living.
Empty eyes. Dead skin. Still wearing
the Mrs. Santa suit. Chained against
the back wall with a long chain.

Ella LEAPS at Calvin, arms out-
stretched, the chain pulling taut
right where that tape line is.

Her eyes again zap with colored
energy.

Calvin is just out of reach, and
doesn't even flinch even though she's
merely inches away.

                    CALVIN (CONT'D)
        So here's what I'm thinking. Santa
        on the roof with his sleigh. Solid
        lights in an outline, but maybe
        blinking lights in the middle that
        spell out like…Merry Christmas,
                    or something.

Ella still straining to get him,
making GROANING SOUNDS. Calvin
thinking.

                    CALVIN (CONT'D)
        Maybe you're right. Now that I

say it, it does sound sort of
lame. I wish I could find the
perfect decoration. Something
that really stands out.

Ella seems to subside noticing the dog
food that's in reach. It's not brains,
but it'll do.

Ella drops down into the bowl, mashing
her face into it as she eats.

The bowl scraping around on the floor
as she laps it up.

CALVIN (CONT'D)
I'll figure it out. I'll just
have to check some places today.
There's a neighborhood near work
I haven't looked at. Hopefully
they'll have something that
inspires me.

Ella looks up. The bowl is empty, but
her hunger is far from gone. Pieces of
dog food dripping from her face.

She leaps at him again, snapping her
teeth. Calvin looks happy. He smiles.

CALVIN (CONT'D)

                    I love you too, honey.

EXT. CALVIN'S YARD - DAY - MOMENTS
LATER

The garage door slowly opens, with the
same RUMBLING, but the vehicle behind
the door is Frank's "beaut," driven by
Calvin. The top on the convertible
is up.

The garage door finally reaches the
top. Calvin slowly pulls out onto his
driveway and stops.

INT. CALVIN'S CONVERTIBLE - CALVIN'S
YARD - DAY - CONTINUOUS

Calvin looks in the rearview mirror.
Notices something on his face and
leans forward, brushing it away.

He nods to himself, and then looks
over at- Mr. Bear seat-belted in,
riding shotgun.

                    CALVIN
          Welp, Mr. Bear. Today's a
               nice day…

He presses a button. The top for the

convertible starts to fold in, letting
in the daylight.

                    CALVIN (CONT'D)
          How about we let the top down?

The top folds into place. Calvin picks
up a pair of shades and puts them on.
Then picks up a smaller pair and puts
them on Mr. Bear.

Mr. Bear is looking good.

Calvin hits a button and the gate at
the street slowly slides open.

EXT. CALVIN'S YARD - DAY - CONTINUOUS

Calvin pulls out and the gate shuts.

Zombie Frank shuffles over to the car.

Calvin spots him and watches him get
closer and closer.

                    CALVIN
          Hey Frank? Anything new?

Frank GROANS and picks up the pace.
He's just close enough now to touch
the car.

Calvin lets off the brake and the car
idles down the street, just fast
enough to stay ahead of Frank.

> CALVIN (CONT'D)
> I'm still taking care of it. No
> worries at all.

Frank GROANS AGAIN.

> CALVIN (CONT'D)
> Yeah, it's tough all over.

Frank keeps trying to get to Calvin as
he slowly glides down the road.

> CALVIN (CONT'D)
> Well, Frank. I got to get to
> work. Don't want to be late.

Calvin presses the accelerator leaving
Frank behind.

Frank tries to follow him down the
road as Calvin makes a turn, heading
out of sight.

EXT. USED CAR LOT - MORNING - MOMENTS
LATER

Rows of cars, all with prices written in the windows.

Signs are stuck in the dirt that read, "Used Cars!"

Calvin getting out of his car, hitting a button under the dash to pop the trunk.

                    CALVIN
          Just sit tight Mr. Bear.

INSERT SHOT: Mr. Bear. doing just that. Seatbelted in. Still rocking the shades.

BACK TO SCENE

Calvin walks around to the back and pulls out duct tape, a gas can, and a rubber hose.

He walks down a line of vehicles that all have a large X with duct tape on the hood.

He gets to the first one in the line without the tape and heads right to the gas tank.

He unscrews the gas can, watching the
end of the parking lot.

A zombie is staggering around between
the vehicles. It hasn't seen Calvin,
but he's keeping an eye on it.

He sticks the hose down the tank and
begins to suck on the other end.

And up it comes, Calvin spitting gas
from his mouth as he jams the hose
into the can to catch the flow.

He holds the hose, still keeping an
eye on the zombie who seems to be
checking out one of the cars.

After the can is full Calvin pulls out
his hose and walks over to the hood.

He pulls out a long strip of duct tape
and presses it down on the hood.

Then a second piece, marking it with a
big X.

The zombie seems to have spotted
Calvin, starting to make a slow, but
steady beeline right for him.

Calvin puts the can in the trunk with
the hose and tape and gets in his car.

He starts the car and pulls right past
the zombie. Calvin waves as he
goes by.

The zombie almost looks confused. His
EYES ZAP.

INT. RADIO STATION - DJ BOOTH -
MORNING - MOMENTS LATER

Calvin's on the mic.

Mr. Bear is there, without shades,
overlooking the radio sound board.

> CALVIN
> Merry Christmas Eve to all my
> listeners. I don't know what the
> weather conditions are going to
> be on this Jolly night, but right
> now it's absolutely beautiful out
> there, and that's really all I
> need to know. We're going to get
> some music playing, but before I
> do just a couple reminders. First
> one's a big one. We are still
> collecting those donations.
> People out there need to eat.

Calvin gets out of his chair, no
longer talking into the mic but still
speaking as if he is, walking over to
the stacks of donations boxes, which
are a lot less than before.
Calvin starts shifting through the
boxes, looking inside.

                    CALVIN (CONT'D)
        We've still got so many boxes and
                    so much tuna.

Calvin pulls out one of the cans of
tuna.

                    CALVIN (CONT'D)
        And let me tell you, it hasn't
        started tasting any better.

Calvin sits back down, opening a
nearby drawer, pulling out a can
opener and starting to open the tuna.

                    CALVIN (CONT'D)
                    (back into the mic)
        But as my buddy Ray says, at
        least people are giving. Nothing
        quite like the Christmas spirit.

Calvin has the tuna open, and pulls a
fork from the drawer.

CALVIN (CONT'D)
And the second is if anyone out
there has any requests. Doesn't
even have to be a Christmas song.
This is your chance to call in
and pick a tune…or just say
hello…

Calvin looks at a phone nearby. No
lights. No anything.

CALVIN (CONT'D)
Literally will play anything…

Still nothing.

CALVIN (CONT'D)
Hey, that's no problem. I'm sure
I can find something for us to
listen to. It is what I do after
all, and no one does it better.
We'll keep the hits going as long
as the generator holds.

Calvin hits a switch and a SONG COMES
ON. Calvin speaks over the intro-

CALVIN (CONT'D)
Here's a good one guys and gals.
This is one of my wife's
favorites.

The MUSIC plays on as Calvin sits so very alone, eating his tuna. Mr. Bear nearby.

EXT. RADIO STATION - PARKING LOT - AFTERNOON - LATER

Calvin coming out of the station carrying Mr. Bear and a can of corn. He locks up behind him.

He's idly shaking his keys as he gets close to what is now his car, the top still down.

He walks over to the passenger side and gets Mr. Bear all belted in.

                    CALVIN
          There we go. All safe.

Calvin walks to the trunk of the car, puts the keys in the lock as—

He HEARS A RIFLE, BLAM!

Calvin jumps. Not because he's scared of a shot, but it's so out of place in his new world.

He peers around and looks for the
source.

Across the road he sees a zombie wandering down the sidewalk, as if it
might be out for a stroll.

It's the only thing moving. He watches
it still looking for answers…and then
it happens-

BLAM!

The zombie's face explodes and down it
goes.

Calvin looks from the direction the
shot came from and sees a man in his
late 50s, GM, holding a rifle with a
scope and a strap hanging from it. The
work shirt he wears has the name
"Karen" stitched on, and a pair of 3-D
glasses are hanging from his neck on a
string.

GM pumps his fist in celebration.

                    GM
                Headshot!

Calvin reacts mostly out of surprise.

                    CALVIN
              (shouting at GM)
              What the hell?!

GM's quick. He cycles the bolt and
chambers another round in seconds and
FIRES off a quick shot toward Calvin.

Calvin dives out of the way as the
bullet knocks a hole in the trunk.

Calvin, still holding the corn, crawls
on his hands and knees putting the car
between them.

                 CALVIN (CONT'D)
            (as he crawls, shouting)
            Don't shoot! Don't shoot!

                      GM
                  (shouting)
              You're alive?

                    CALVIN
                  (shouting)
        I'm talking to you, aren't I?

                      GM
                  (shouting)
        I don't want to shoot you. But I
                     will.

GM cycles the rifle again and watches the car through the scope.

>   GM (CONT'D)
>   (shouting)
>   Toss any weapons you got over
>   there.

POV THE SCOPE, looking at movement be-hind the car.

The can of corn arcs over the car and into the lot, GM keeping it in his sights.

BACK TO SCENE

GM looks kind of stunned.

>   GM (CONT'D)
>   (shouting)
>   Did you just throw corn?

>   CALVIN
>   (shouting back)
>   It's all I have.

GM lowers his rifle as Calvin stands with his hands up. GM starts cau-tiously walking over.

GM

There's snappers everywhere and
you're out here with corn?

CALVIN

Snappers?

GM has crossed the gap and is not far
from Calvin now.

GM

Fancy name for the living
impaired strolling the streets. I
came up with it. Copyright is
pending so don't steal it.

CALVIN

I don't want to hurt these
people. They're my friends.

GM sticks his arm through the strap
and swings the rifle onto his back.
GM hooks a thumb back toward the
snapper he blasted.

GM

That dude was your friend?

Calvin drops his hands.

CALVIN

75

That was Bert, out for his jog.

GM turns around and looks toward the dead zombie, laying in an uncomfortable pile.

                    GM
        Must be resting up for the next
                   mile.

                  CALVIN
          Don't joke like that.

                    GM
        I'm sorry if you knew him before,
        but he's dead kid. Snapper city.

                  CALVIN
        I didn't know him before. He just
            looked like a Bert.

GM studies Calvin. He's not sure if he's a looney.

                    GM
          You from that nuthouse?

                  CALVIN
          The mental facility?

                    GM

Not that there's anything wrong
with that. I've met some of those
guys.

                    CALVIN
     No. I just…I'm not crazy. It's
              just…easier.

GM understands.

                    GM
     You know what. I get that.

GM decides to start over, offers his
hand.

                    GM (CONT'D)
     Name's GM. Sorry I shot…Bert.

                    CALVIN
              (pointing at the name)
     Your shirt says Karen.

                    GM
     Not my shirt.

Calvin considers, then takes his hand
and they shake.

                    CALVIN
     Calvin. I work…worked, at the

                    station here.

                         GM
          A DJ, huh? I worked on a garbage
                       truck.

GM leans against the car.

                    GM (CONT'D)
          After the shit went down, just
          kept doing what I knew. Going
          door to door. Taking out the
                      trash.

                      CALVIN
                      Trash?

                         GM
          Well, it's more like during the
          black plague. They'd come around
          and yell, "bring out the dead,"
          and they'd…bring out the dead.

Calvin walks around to the trunk.

                    GM (CONT'D)
          But now when I say it, they come
          shuffling out on their own two
                       feet.

Calvin sees the gunshot hole in the

trunk and walks over to it, rubbing
the metal.

                    CALVIN
                    Oh no.

                    GM
          Oh yeah. Sorry about that.

                    CALVIN
          Frank's going to be pissed.

                    GM
          He a friend or a...
          (GM motions at Bert)
          friend?

                    CALVIN
          He...was my neighbor. I just like
          to remember him as he was.

                    GM
          Well, you don't have to pretend
                    any more.

GM extends his arms, and Calvin actually jumps at the chance to hug him,
almost knocking GM over. It's been a
while for human contact.

                    GM (CONT'D)

                                              79

It was more of a gesture than an
invitation. Calvin steps back.

                    CALVIN
          So, what now?

                    GM
     I could use a hand loading Bert
          in my truck.

                    CALVIN
          In a garbage truck?

                    GM
     That piece of shit quit working a
          while back.

EXT. NEARBY LOT - AFTERNOON - MOMENTS
LATER

Calvin and GM, carrying the body of
what was "Bert" to the back of a beat-
up pickup truck.

The inside is full of other dead snappers. Flies buzz about. Bert's pretty
heavy, but they manage after some
struggling. GM shuts the tailgate.

                    GM
     So, I'm just going to drop these

snappers in the dump, set'em on
fire, and then head back
this way.

GM hops in the truck and tries to
start it.

Calvin leans into the passenger window, a duffle bag sits on the passenger side.

> GM (CONT'D)
> After that, my schedule's pretty
> open.

GM notices the truck's not turning
over.

> GM (CONT'D)
> Well shit. I was hoping to get a
> little more out of this thing.

> CALVIN
> So what now?

GM reaches into the duffle bag. We see
all matters of guns, water bottles,
and ammo inside.

> GM
> I've always got a plan B.

He rummages inside the bag a little
more, and then he holds up a grenade,
showing it to Calvin.

>   GM (CONT'D)
>   Voila. Plan B.

Calvin looks at GM, concerned and
confused.

GM grabs his duffle and jumps out of
the truck. He walks around and hands
the bag to Calvin.

>   GM (CONT'D)
>   Now, if you'd be so kind as to move
>   a bit.

Calvin takes a couple steps.

>   GM (CONT'D)
>   No, really move.

Calvin takes another step. GM points
into the distance.

>   GM (CONT'D)
>   Far.

Calvin does as he's told.

                    GM (CONT'D)
              (yelling across the distance)
          And stay out of my way. I'm about
              to haul ass, and I haul a lot
                       of ass.

Calvin weakly gives a thumbs up.

GM gets a giant grin across his face
as he holds up the grenade and-

PULLS THE PIN tossing it into the back
of the truck.

GM does exactly as advertised, and
starts hauling ass over to Calvin.

He makes it to him and covers his
ears, turning around to watch.

Calvin drops the bag and does the same.
A beat.

GM takes a step forward and looks confused. He turns toward Calvin.

                    GM (CONT'D)
                 Guess it was a-

BOOOOM!

GM jumps in surprise as an explosion of arms, eyes, legs, and everything else that makes up a snapper leap into the air as the shock wave ECHOES.

The parts rain around GM and Calvin.

> CALVIN
> Not exactly a respectful burial.

The head of Bert lands and rolls past them.

> GM
> There's a snag now and then.

INT. CALVIN'S CONVERTIBLE - THE STATION - EVENING - LATER

Calvin climbing into his car.

The top is still folded down.

Calvin puts his corn on the seat between him and Mr. Bear. The passenger door suddenly opens and there's GM.

GM sees Mr. Bear and hesitates.

> CALVIN
> You're riding with me?

GM

Well you just saw me blow what's
left of my truck to hell.
Figured I'd stick with you
a bit.

CALVIN
I guess that's okay.

GM
You have something planned?

CALVIN
Just going home to have dinner
with my wife.

GM
Your wife? Oh shit. Can't get
away from them even after the end
of the world.

GM looks at Mr. Bear.

CALVIN
Oh. Right.

Calvin grabs Mr. Bear and pulls him
free of the seat belt, and sets him in
the backseat.

He pulls the belt over, picks up the

shades and puts them on Mr. Bear
again.
GM just looks at him.

                    GM
     And you're sure you didn't live
          in that facility, right?

                  CALVIN
          It was my daughter's.

GM takes the hint.

                    GM
                    Ah.

GM climbs in.

              GM (CONT'D)
        Let's go meet the misses.

EXT. MENTAL HEALTH FACILITY - EVENING

Large fences around a large building.
A large sign on the gate once read,
"Mud Creek Mental Facility," but had
been repainted over in a suspiciously
dried blood red and brown, to say, "TO
SERVE JESUS."

There's a small shed nearby the front

gate and a guard booth. And there
sits BOB.

Bob's wearing an orange jumpsuit. The
back reads, "Mud Creek Mental
Facility."

Bob's rifle is propped in the corner
near him. In front of him sits a
pistol that's been taken apart. He's
cleaning and putting it back together.
Not in a rush. Meticulous.

Inside are several others. They look
normal enough other than the orange
jumpsuits. They're playing a game of
freeze tag. Taking turns chasing each
other and "freezing."

ANDY, wild eyed and also wearing the
orange, a holstered pistol hanging
from his belt, walks over to Bob's
booth.

                    ANDY
     Hey Bob. It is Bob, right? Or
      Robert, maybe? Bob doesn't
               respond.

              ANDY (CONT'D)
     I'm gonna stick with Bob. Any

who. Me and Wes are gonna go out
for a drive later. Maybe check
some houses. Blow shit up.

Bob still doesn't look up. Just keeps
cleaning the pistol.

           ANDY (CONT'D)
    You want me to pick you up
      something? Anything in a
    wrapper's usually still good.
        Like a honey bun?

Still no response.

           ANDY (CONT'D)
  I didn't know how much I'd want a
  banana till I couldn't have one.
   You know what I mean? Still,
   selection's better for us now
     though than when we were
         locked up.

Andy whacks Bob's shoulder as he
laughs.

Bob reaches down and snatches the
rifle from where it was, startling
Andy.

Bob points the gun outside the fence,
and pulls the trigger with a BLAM!

Out in the field, a snapper, now with
a hole for a nose, drops to the
ground.

Bob props the rifle back up in the
corner.

                    ANDY (CONT'D)
          Damn that's fast shooting. I'm
          pretty quick, too. Watch this.

Bob indulges, turning to watch.

Andy drops into a gunfighter stance
and narrows his eyes. He wiggles his
fingers above the butt of his pistol.

He looks out at a sign in the
distance.

                    ANDY (CONT'D)
          Calling the shot. Right through
          the middle of that sign.

Fingers wiggle more. And then-

He slaps leather pulling his piece,

but barely clears his belt, firing a
shot into the ground.

Andy jumps back terrified, dropping
the gun.

Bob looks at Andy a moment and turns
back to what he was doing. Andy re-
gains his composure and starts
laughing like a mad man.

> ANDY (CONT'D)
> I am just TOO fast! Did you see
> how fast I was? Wow.

Bob has finished his assembly and
picks the gun up and racks the slide.

> ANDY (CONT'D)
> I'm gonna let ya get back to it.

Andy picks up his pistol, jams it back
in his holster, and wanders off.

INT. CALVIN'S CAR - DRIVING - EVENING

Back with Calvin and GM in the car,
cruising along.

> GM

I have to say, I'm glad I didn't
shoot you.

CALVIN
You and I both.

GM
Last guy I met wasn't too bad. He
seemed a little slow. And a
little too happy to wish the old
world goodbye. But these days
when it comes to friends, beggars
can't be choosers. Ya know?

GM whacks Calvin's shoulder.

GM (CONT'D)
Ask your buddy Bert what I mean.

CALVIN
I can't.

GM
Exactly. He's a snapper that you
didn't even know.

CALVIN
No, I mean, I can't because you
shot him in the face and blew
him up.

                    GM
        Oh right. Guess he wouldn't be
              all that chatty.

Calvin gives him a look.

                 GM (CONT'D)
        So what about you? How're you
           spending your apocalypse?

                   CALVIN
        At first I told myself I might
          find more people if I kept
           broadcasting on the radio.

Calvin shakes his head.

                CALVIN (CONT'D)
        I guess now I just go out of
                   habit.

GM looks at him.

                    GM
        That's some sad shit. The end of
          the world comes knocking and
         you're still punching a clock.

                   CALVIN
        I just like the routine. I get
        gas for generators. Head to work.

> And then look for Christmas
> decorations.

                    GM
> Christmas decorations? It's
>   like…

GM counts on his fingers.

                GM (CONT'D)
>   …June.

                  CALVIN
>   I know.

                    GM
> So you just love Christmas that
>   much?

                  CALVIN
>   I fucking hate it.

                    GM
>   Oh.

EXT. CALVIN'S NEIGHBORHOOD - EVENING -
MOMENTS LATER

Calvin pulls into his cul-de-sac, and
there blocking the middle of the road
is Ray. He looks rough. The Christmas

tree hat worn and bent. His outfit
still stained with blood.

Ray slowly makes his way toward the
car, still has that same limp. His
EYES ZAPPING like Ella's.

Calvin is watching Ray as he passes by
on the passenger side.

GM unexpectedly throws his door open
hitting Ray and sending him flying,
rolling down the road.

                    CALVIN
          What the hell are you doing?

                    GM
          How many points? A hundred?

Ray's spins to a stop. His
EYES ZAP.

INT. CALVIN'S HOUSE - GARAGE - EVENING
- CONTINUOUS

Calvin pulls in and parks the car.
He's annoyed.

GM is looking at him, not sure what
to say.

Calvin collects his thoughts and
speaks-

> CALVIN
> I know it's hard to understand,
> but Ray was my friend.

GM takes a moment to respond.

> GM
> So…two hundred?

Calvin can't believe him.

> GM (CONT'D)
> Look, look. I'm just joking
> around. You have your ways to
> deal. I have mine.

> CALVIN
> I know…It's just…Ray. We used to
> work together. Play chess.

> GM
> Y'all play much chess now?

> CALVIN
> …No.

> GM
> Why? Does he cheat?

95

Calvin reluctantly grins a bit. His
sanity is still in there. He considers
a moment.

                    CALVIN
     I know what you're trying to say.

Calvin climbs out of the car. He leans
back in and looks at GM.

               CALVIN (CONT'D)
               You hungry?

                    GM
               I could eat.

INT. CALVIN'S HOUSE - LIVING ROOM -
EVENING - MOMENTS LATER

The fake Christmas tree still in
place, but not lit up.

GM is sitting on the couch by himself
holding an empty can of food and a
fork.

He scraps around the can and then
peers inside. Nothing.

He starts looking around the room at
the tree and then the spot on the wall

where Ray's blood was, noticeably
cleaner than the area around it.

GM stands up and walks around.

He sets his empty can down as he walks
over to the tree, touching some of the
ornaments.

INSERT GM LOOKING AT: an ornament
that's a picture of Calvin, Ella, and
Tina all posing near the same tree.
Ella wearing the Santa outfit. Calvin
not paying attention. Tina holding Mr.
Bear.

BACK TO SCENE

GM looks down and sees the plug near
the outlet, reaches down, plugs
it in.

Lights shine, bringing the tree back
to life.

GM takes a moment to enjoy the colors.
A SCRAPING NOISE from Ella's bowl
turns his attention away.

INT. CALVIN'S HOUSE - BEDROOM -
EVENING - CONTINUOUS

97

Calvin is sitting, back to the door,
near Ella who's once again face down
in her pink bowl.

He has his can of corn, which he's
eating with a spoon as he talks.

                    CALVIN
                (quietly to Ella)
    ...just like always. Walking out to
        my car and there he was.

GM pokes his head in and sees Ella.

He has a moment of surprise, but then
sort of shakes his head and takes a
step inside.

                CALVIN (CONT'D)
                  (quietly)
          He seems nice, though.

Calvin pauses like he's hearing a
response.

                CALVIN (CONT'D)
    ...I don't know yet. He did shoot
            Bert in the face.

Ella looks up like she's reacting to
the conversation-

Her EYES ZAP as she starts to chew and
drops back into the bowl.

> GM
> Sooo…that's the little
> woman, huh?

Calvin doesn't even look back.

> GM (CONT'D)
> And you feed her…dog food?

> CALVIN
> She has…digestive issues.

Calvin sits another moment, puts his
can of corn down and walks out
past GM.

GM starts to follow and then turns
back and looks at Ella who is looking
back.

> GM
> Nice to meet you, ma'am.

GM considers for a second if this is
strange, then turns to leave.

INT. CALVIN'S HOUSE - LIVING ROOM -
EVENING - CONTINUOUS

As GM is walking into the living
room, Calvin is standing next to the
plugged in tree, glowing with
Christmas cheer.

They both stand in silence a moment.

                    CALVIN
        I know it's different, but we
             have it worked out.

                    GM
              If you say so.

GM goes and sits down on the couch.

                    CALVIN
           You think it's odd?

                    GM
        Welllll. She's dead. Wants to
        kill you and eat your face and
        you've chained her up and are
        feeding her dog food out of a
        pretty little dog bowl. Nothing
        odd about that and don't let
        anyone tell you different.

Calvin thinks.

                    CALVIN

But maybe there will be a cure.
Ya know?

GM
For being dead? I don't think so.
You don't get over that.

CALVIN
This isn't dead, this is
something else.

GM
Well, if it's not dead, it's one
step away from it. And if one of
those snappers gets a hold of us,
we will be too. You get that jolt
and you're never the same.

CALVIN
I still don't even know what
happened to her. What happened to
everyone. I was just in the
garage and…

GM
Well that's why.

Calvin looks at him confused.

GM (CONT'D)
You didn't see the lights.

                    CALVIN
        Lights? The last thing Ella said
           was something about lights.

                     GM
        Yeah man. I was watching a 3-D
        movie. I like'em. I think they're
                coming back...

FLASHBACK

INT. GM'S HOUSE - LIVING ROOM - NIGHT
- SIX MONTHS AGO

GM is sitting on the couch in his
living room. He has on those same 3-D
glasses and some pajamas with cartoon
characters on them.

                   GM (O.S.)
        I started seeing these flashes of
                   color.

EXT. GM'S YARD - NIGHT - CONTINUOUS

GM walks out onto his porch wearing
the 3-D glasses still, looking up into
the sky as the same colored lightening
from before lights up the sky like
fireworks.

GM (O.S.)
It was over as quick as it
started.

END OF FLASHBACK

INT. CALVIN'S HOUSE - LIVING ROOM -
NIGHT - PRESENT DAY

GM now wearing the 3-D glasses that
were hanging from his neck.

GM
These babies saved my life.

Calvin points next to the tree.

CALVIN
The night it happened, I found
Ella and my daughter, Tina, here,
on the ground…not breathing.

GM
That's what I mean by dead,
Calvin.

CALVIN
Next thing I knew, Tina had
gotten out. Bit Ray. And Ray…

Calvin doesn't want to continue. GM
takes off the glasses.

> GM
> I'm sure he had no choice.

Calvin reaches down and pulls the
plug on the tree. The tree goes
dark.

> CALVIN
> Before I knew it, everyone that
> meant anything to me was ripped
> away.

INSERT: CALVIN'S YARD

A little mound of dirt on the far
corner.

> CALVIN (O.S.) (CONT'D)
> After it all went down, I buried
> Tina in the yard. But Ella was
> still…whatever she is.

> GM
> She's dead Calvin.

> CALVIN
> She's not dead! I told you. This
> is…something else.

GM
You know she wouldn't want to
live like that.

CALVIN
You don't know what she wants.

GM
Would you want to live like that?

Calvin turns away.

CALVIN
I just...can't.

GM
Hey. I'm not trying to push you,
but you know these things rot.
Eventually it's going to happen.

CALVIN
But if they eat...or are...fed. They
seem to last longer.

GM
That's not your wife in there.
And feeding her dog food is not
going to change that. Shit, they
haven't been human in six months.
Closest they ever get is when
they hear the music.

Calvin looks at him confused.

>   GM (CONT'D)
>   Oh hell, you don't know.

>   CALVIN
>   Know what?

GM only grins.

EXT. RANDOM HOUSE - ROOFTOP - NIGHT -
MOMENTS LATER

GM is crawling up a ladder onto the
roof of a house with his bag.

Calvin is right behind him.

>   CALVIN
>   I don't know why you couldn't
>   just tell me.

>   GM
>   Can someone just tell you about
>   the Grand Canyon? Or tell you
>   about a sunset.

GM pulls the ladder up behind him.

>   CALVIN
>   Sure.

                    GM
     Of course not. Look. Just sit
     down and prepare to be amazed.

Calvin reluctantly takes a seat,
watching GM.

GM shifts through his bag and comes
out with a portable music player with
speakers.

                GM (CONT'D)
           Prepare yourself.

GM dramatically hits the button- But
nothing happens.

                  CALVIN
                 Amazing.

GM hits the button again.

                    GM
     Ah hell. I haven't charged it.

GM goes through his bag again.

                  CALVIN
           You going to blow it up?

                    GM

What? No.

GM pulls out a small portable charger.

GM (CONT'D)
I think I still have a little
charge left in this buddy.

He plugs his player into the charger
and again hits the button.

It comes to life, MUSIC STARTS and GM
sets it down next to him.

The DEAD BEAT. Strong drumbeats that
echoes into the night.

Calvin is waiting on something. Anything. He looks at GM.

CALVIN
What exactly are we-

GM whacks Calvin's shoulder and then
points.

A couple snappers have rounded the
corner of a nearby house, shuffling
toward the house.

Then a couple more.

Before long, there's more than a
dozen, all standing in the yard,
swaying to the music.
Calvin looks at GM.

GM points again, not wanting Calvin to
miss it.

                    GM
            Look, look, look.

The MUSIC BEATS as the SNAPPERS JAM,
twisting and jumping to the music.

There's no coordination, but they're
certainly getting down.

GM is swaying and jiving while he
sits, grinning as he enjoys the
moment.

Calvin's actually grinning as well.

                  CALVIN
            This IS amazing.

GM laughs.

                    GM
        I found it out by accident.

109

                    CALVIN
          They even look happy.

                      GM
          They're still snappy little
          snappers, but as long as the
          music has their attention, they
          seem to forget about the hunger.

GM thinks a moment.

                  GM (CONT'D)
          Sometimes I like to pick them off
          with a rifle. I mean, I feel a
          little guilty about it, but…

They both watch a moment.

                  GM (CONT'D)
          But they hate it when the music
          turns off. Gets them fired up.
          Stronger and hungrier than before.

GM hits a button and the snappers
grind to a halt, and all turn toward
Calvin and GM on the roof.

In unison they all start running at
the side of the house. More agitated
than ever seen before. ANIMAL LIKE

SNARLS from below. Their EYES ZAPPING.
Slamming against the walls.

It's a real moment of chaos, and de-
spite the safety of the roof, Calvin
looks mighty worried.

GM doesn't mind. He looks at them
throwing themselves at them and lets
out a big laugh.

               GM (CONT'D)
           (loudly at the snappers)
         They are pissed now!

GM turns the music back on and the
snappers all fall back into the
groove.

We stay with the undead a bit. Let
them do their thing.

We pull away from GM's dance party
and, without going far, come to find-

EXT. MENTAL HEALTH FACILITY - NIGHT -
CONTINUOUS

It's close enough the BASS OF GM'S
MUSIC can almost be heard thumping.

In the guard booth, there is no Bob.
Only Andy and now WES, a weasel
looking guy in one of the orange jumpsuits. He's leaning on the booth.

Andy's sitting in Bob's chair, leaned
back, his feet kicked up on the table.

He has Bob's rifle, peering down the
sights of it at nothing in particular.

There's a BANGING coming from the
shed.

> WES
> How long you gotta be on guard
> duty?

> ANDY
> Reverend said all night.

> WES
> That's dumb.

Andy and Wes both sit there as the
BANGING from the shed continues.

Andy sets the rifle down and lets out
an exasperated sigh.

> ANDY

I'm so bored. I'm starting to go
crazy just sitting here. You hear
music, or is it just me?

They both stop to listen. The music's
there, but the BANGING continues.

                    WES
I can't hear nothing over those
things being loud as hell
                  tonight.

                   ANDY
They're loud as hell every night.

Wes starts to walk over to the shed.

              ANDY (CONT'D)
Don't get near them things.

                    WES
Seem louder than usual.

Wes slowly makes his way to the shed.

He gets to one of the windows and
peers inside.

               WES (CONT'D)
Come look at this one. He looks
like he's dancing.

                    ANDY
        Them things don't dance. They eat
        and that's it. Wes still looking
                    inside.

                    WES
          Aww shit. He stopped doing it.

                    ANDY
             They don't dance.
        Wes BANGS his hand against the
                    shed.

                    WES
               Dance, dummy!

        Wes listens. The MUSIC has stopped,
        but the banging is worse. Wes whacks
        the shed again.

                 WES (CONT'D)
            Y'all shut up in there!

        Wes shrugs his shoulders and walks
        back over to the booth.

                 WES (CONT'D)
          In the morning you ain't gotta
                 guard any more?

                    ANDY

That's what The Reverend said.

                    WES
You wanna go find something to do
          after breakfast?

                   ANDY
                   Can't.

                    WES
Thought you only had to be here
        during the night.

                   ANDY
        I can't because…

Andy points at Bob on the floor of the
booth. Bob has a bullet hole in the
back of his head and is very much
dead. His head in a pool of dried
blood and a few brain pieces.

               ANDY (CONT'D)
I gotta take this stupid som'
     bitch out and bury him.

                    WES
Want me to come with ya?

                   ANDY
Reverend said I gotta do it

                    myself.
                (mocking tone)
        Said if I'm gonna learn not to
        shoot people, I gotta take
        responsibility for what I did.

Andy whacks Bob's dead corpse with his
foot.

                    WES
        What'd Bob do? Said something
        about you the way you shoot?

                    ANDY
        Didn't say nothing. Didn't have
        to. I know what he was thinking.

Andy kicks at Bob's body again.

INT. CALVIN'S HOUSE - KITCHEN - NIGHT
- LATER

Calvin and GM come in through the
garage into the kitchen.

On the fridge is a calendar of June
with several Xs over dates leading up
to the 23. Under those Xs all say
CHRISTMAS EVE!

                    CALVIN

(to himself)
Did it again.

Calvin crosses out the 23 and writes
Christmas Eve on tomorrow's date.
June 24.

GM watches this all go down without a
word.

Calvin drops the marker and opens the
fridge.

He grabs a couple bottles of beer and
hands one to GM.

Calvin looks upset as he heads into
the living room.

GM looks at the calendar, then sees a
pile just like it nearby. January,
February, all the way up to May.

All the dates say Christmas Eve. All
with Xs. GM looks toward where Calvin
left.

EXT. CALVIN'S YARD - NIGHT - MOMENTS
LATER

Snappers line the fence outside. The

night seems to be when they are most active, pawing at the fence, and snapping their teeth. The occasional ZAP OF THEIR EYES light up the darkness.

Calvin is laying back in a lawn chair, looking at the sky, holding that beer.

GM is dragging a small cooler near Calvin, still holding his own beer.

Calvin notices.

                    CALVIN
        Sorry about that. Just have the
        one chair. Didn't really have use
                for another.

                    GM
            That's good to hear.

                    CALVIN
                How's that?

                    GM
        That you actually do understand
          Ray's not moments away from
        coming to hang. I've been trying
        to decide if you actually had a
        real handle on what's going on.

GM is close to Calvin now and takes a
seat on the cooler.

                    GM (CONT'D)
        No judgement. As I said, pickings
           for amigos out here have been
                       slim.

Calvin takes a look at the fence and
sees Ray, SNAPPING AND ZAPPING.

                    CALVIN
        I do know. I know allll too well.

                      GM
        I gotta ask…what's the deal with
        you and Christmas? You mentioned
        Christmas lights before. And just
             now with the calendar…

                    CALVIN
          It's my wife. She loved
        Christmas. Her and my daughter
        both. And every year I'd say,
        this is the year I do it big. But
        time would get away from me. And
           every year I'd say, there's
               always next time.

Calvin takes a sip.

                    CALVIN (CONT'D)
          I am fresh out of next times.

                         GM
          So why haven't you done it? The
          hustle and bustle of day-to-day
          life is pretty much your doing.

                       CALVIN
          I'm still looking for the right
          decorations. If I'm going to do
          this, the final Christmas for
          them, I want it to be perfect.

                         GM
          Lights are lights. I mean, at the
          end of the day the choices are-
                 (counts on his fingers)
          -lights, reindeers, a fat dude
          in a red suit, and presents.
          Maybe a few Jesi if that's your
                        thing.

                       CALVIN
                        Jesi?

                         GM
          That's plural for Jesus.

                       CALVIN
          I just want it to be perfect.

GM

It's the apocalypse! What perfect
are you going to find in little
twinkling lights? You want to
know what I think?

CALVIN

Not really.

GM

You don't go through with it
because once you do, it's all
over. The whole Christmas thing
has been over for six months, but
the moment the lights come on and
nothing's different, then what?

Calvin notices he's leaned back as if
on a couch, with GM sitting nearby.

CALVIN

What are you, a psychiatrist?

GM

Wanted to be. Went to classes and
everything, actually. But I get
easily distracted - mainly by
women.

CALVIN

That can happen.

GM

I liked meeting women. Just
didn't like getting to know
them.

CALVIN

Relationships can be hard.

GM

Especially yours.

CALVIN

That was the agreement. Through
sickness and health.

GM

Also till death do you part, but
that hasn't slowed you down.

GM and Calvin both take a sip.

GM (CONT'D)

Who am I to judge? At least you
had someone. Had time with her.
Your wife and your daughter. Me?
I had a cat. And I hated that
son-of-a- bitch. You know the way
they stretch their leg out and
lick their balls?

CALVIN

Pretty gross.

                    GM
          Hell, I was jealous.

Calvin laughs.

                  CALVIN
     I know it all sounds odd. But I
     just want to do this for Ella.

                    GM
     You think Ella would care if she
          knew what happened?

                  CALVIN
     I'm trying to keep a promise.

                    GM
     But you don't. It's six months in
     and nothing is different.

A beat.

               GM (CONT'D)
     How about this? Tomorrow, you and
     I find those perfect decorations.
     Just deck the hell out of these
     halls and then we'll see what
               happens next.

EXT. UNKNOWN NEIGHBORHOODS - MORNING -
THE NEXT DAY

A MONTAGE of Calvin's truck cruising.
The bed of it empty until-

They start pulling into different dri-
veways and loading all sorts of
Christmas lawn decorations into the
back.

Happy little snowmen, a ton of lights,
a few Jesi, and enough reindeer for
Santa to start his own airline, all
start to fill the bed of the truck.

END MONTAGE

EXT. ANOTHER HOUSE IN AN UNKNOWN
NEIGHBORHOOD - CONTINUOUS

GM and Calvin are working to pull some
lights down off the side of the house.

In the background, a snapper has
rounded the corner wearing a Santa
outfit.

Snapper Santa trudges closer and
closer, both GM and Calvin unaware,
too focused on the task at hand.

He's close now, and starts to zero in
on Calvin.

GM effortlessly pulls a revolver from his waistband and executes Snapper Santa, the bullet going straight into the Santa hat.

Snapper Santa crumples as Calvin jumps, surprised, then looks at GM annoyed.

                    CALVIN
      I wish you'd stop doing that.

                      GM
                    What?

EXT. UNKNOWN HOUSE IN AN UNKNOWN NEIGHBORHOOD - MOMENTS LATER

Calvin and GM are working together to carry a plastic snowman the same way they loaded Bert before. GM now wearing the hat Snapper Santa had. It has a hole in it from the bullet.

They get Frosty tucked into the back, GM wiggling it into place on top of everything else, wedging it into the pile.

Calvin's gaze is fixated on a house across the road. GM hasn't noticed.

                    GM
    We should have brought something
        to tie all this stuff down.

GM picks up some of the Christmas
lights.

                GM (CONT'D)
        Could use lights maybe to…

GM sees Calvin looking distracted at
the house across the way.

                GM (CONT'D)
        You alright there, bud?

Calvin walks across the road.

                GM (CONT'D)
                Calvin?

EXT. ANOTHER HOUSE - MORNING - CON-
TINUOUS

Calvin approaches the red leg of a
towering Santa display, big enough it
could jump onto the roof if it so
chose.

Calvin is starry eyed, GM walking up
behind him.

GM

Ho, ho, holy shit.

EXT. CALVIN'S YARD - EVENING - LATER

Calvin's yard. It's full of decorations. Nothing set up. They're just
everywhere.

Calvin and GM are leaning the giant
Santa against the house. GM is still
wearing the hat.

GM

If you had asked me, hey GM,
after the world ends and snappers
roam the lands, what do you
expect to be doing with your
time?
(turning to respond to himself)
Well, other GM...you still look
handsome as ever, by the way.
(turning back)
Well, I do try to take care of
myself.
(turning back)
And it shows!

GM pauses to think.

GM (CONT'D)

> I forget where I was going with
> this.

Calvin isn't listening. He's admiring
everything. He actually looks happy.

GM notices.

> GM (CONT'D)
> Well, bud. Perfect, right?

Calvin's smile starts to fade.

> GM (CONT'D)
> What's happening there with your
> face? I thought this was perfect.

> CALVIN
> It's not bad...

> GM
> Not bad? Christ, man. What else
> could you want short of someone
> dressed as Santa squeezing down
> your chimney? And I'm not
> offering.

GM whips off the Santa hat and puts it
on top of the head of a plastic reindeer nearby.

CALVIN

It's almost perfect.

GM looking around.

GM

Well, it can't be decorations.
This is everything worth bringing
for four whole blocks.

CALVIN

Music.

GM

Music?

CALVIN

We'd listen to Christmas music.
Usually while we rode around and
looked at other people's lights
since ours were never up.

GM

So throw on some tunes. We can
use my player. It just needs to
charge a bit.

CALVIN

I have plenty of music at the
station. In the morning we can

129

> put some music on a timer, get
> the decorations all set up...

                    GM
Probably not going to come across
a Christmas turkey, but we can
find a can of pork N' beans and a
bottle of cheap wine and bring in
the new year. Well, the same
year, new you. Right?

EXT. RADIO STATION - DJ BOOTH -
MORNING

Calvin is pressing buttons on his console while GM pokes around inside.

MUSIC comes on and Calvin hits a
couple buttons.

                    CALVIN
After we pick some songs, we can
set it up to come on and play
nonstop until we turn it off.

GM reaches up to hit a couple random
buttons and Calvin whacks his hand
away.

GM gives him a look.

                    GM
Another computer takes the job of
      the hardworking DJ.

                  CALVIN
You joke, but it's true. Well it
was. It was getting harder to
justify being here other than to
take requests. And I'm pretty
sure they were finding a way for
   people to do that through the
              internet.

                    GM
   Looks like you got the last
            laugh.

                  CALVIN
Not many requests coming in on
      the phone either.

GM and Calvin take a moment as reality
looms.

             CALVIN (CONT'D)
When we get this set up, I'd like
      Ella to be present.

                    GM
            How present.

> CALVIN
> This is all for her.

> GM
> Calvin, she wouldn't know the
> difference between Christmas and
> an ass wiping.

> CALVIN
> We can talk about it later. How
> 'bout this? Make a request! I
> haven't gotten one in so long.

> GM
> Paperback Writer by The Beatles?

> CALVIN
> I don't actually have any
> Beatles.

GM shakes his head.

> GM
> This is why radio is dead.
> Nothing to do with snappers.

> CALVIN
> I got a song by Kasey Lansdale.

> GM
> It's not the Beatles…but sure.

Calvin hits a button—

EXT. USED CAR LOT - MORNING - CON-
TINUOUS

It's Andy and Wes, wandering around
the lot.

Andy's spinning around one of the,
"used car" flags, like a child with a
sparkler, a couple rows over.

Wes is looking at the vehicles with
the Duct Tape Xs.

In the parking lot is Frank, shambling
about, making his way toward Andy.

                    WES
          Andy. What you think these Xs
                  is for?

                    ANDY
          Who gives a shit? Let's blow
                  one up.

Frank is close, gaining speed, eyes
ZAPPING. Andy still waving the flag
around.

                ANDY (CONT'D)

We can put Bob in one and blow it
to smithereens.

Seconds before Andy becomes snapper
chow, Andy spins and drives the flag
right into Frank's head.

Frank stops like he's considering the
mysteries of the universe, his eyes
ZAP once more and then he crumples to
the ground, flag sticking straight
up.

                    WES
The hell's a smithereen, any way?

                    ANDY
It's like an Irish word that
       means little bits.

They're both a little stunned Andy
might be right.

                    ANDY (CONT'D)
       Let's blow up Bob!

ANGLE OVER FRANK, Andy and Wes high
five and laugh.

INT. RANDOM CAR - MORNING - MOMENTS
LATER

Bob's seat-belted into the driver's seat.

They've tied Bob's hands to the steering wheel at ten and two.

Andy and Wes lean back to take a look at their handwork.

> WES
> That's gonna look so cool.

> ANDY
> Yeah. We can pour a bunch of gas on him, and…

Andy simulates an explosion with his hands as he says-

> ANDY (CONT'D)
> Boooooom!

Andy and Wes both laugh.

> WES
> I got an idea. What if we jam the pedal down and make it look like Bob's driving it while it's on fire.

> ANDY

Wes, you're a genius! That's the
best idea I've ever heard.

Wes yanks the cover off the steering
wheel and goes to hot-wiring the
truck.

Wes working away while he speaks.

                    WES
You gonna get in trouble for not
        burying Bob good?

                   ANDY
    The Reverend ain't gonna know
        about it so who cares.

Wes stops fiddling and sits up,
looking dead serious.

                    WES
    I just don't want to make him
    mad. I'm already worried he's
gonna find out I'm out here with
    you. He gets so mad sometimes
                and…

                   ANDY
    He ain't gonna find out.

Wes hesitates a moment and then goes

back to the wires. The car cranks up,
and the MUSIC FROM THE RADIO comes on.

CALVIN (O.S.)
…and I couldn't be happier. So
let me once again say MERRY
CHRISTMAS from all of us here at
K.Z.O.M. radio.

Wes and Andy both look at each other.

CALVIN (O.S.) (CONT'D)
I'm excited to play the first
request I've had in a long time
by my new buddy here, GM. Perhaps
there's a message you'd like to
tell all the listeners out there
in Mud Creek?

ANDY
Mud Creek?

GM (O.S.)
Merry Christmas all you snappers!
Can I press this button?

CALVIN
Don't touch any of them.

GM
I'm sorry to report Calvin here

137

            doesn't have any Beatles. And he
           won't let me press any of the
                  buttons.

                      CALVIN (O.S.)
                 But we do have-

The MUSIC kicks on.

EXT. USED CAR LOT - MORNING - CON-
TINUOUS

Andy steps out onto the lot and looks
down road into the distance where the
station's call letters, KZOM can be
seen. The used car sign sticks up
nearby.

Calvin can be heard from the radio
still, setting up the song.

Wes steps out behind Andy.

                      CALVIN (O.S.)
              And for all you snappers
            listening, hope you're ready,
          because after this song, it's
         going to be Christmas music for
              24 hours straight!

                        WES

You think maybe it's like a
recording?

CALVIN (O.S.)
This is Calvin-

GM (O.S.) (butting in)
And GM…

Andy reaches down and pulls the sign
from Frank, pulling it free. Then
looks out toward the station.

CALVIN
-with K.Z.O.M., wishing everyone
out there, their very own,
perfect Christmas.

Andy fixated on the station.

ANDY
Only one way to find out.

INT. RADIO STATION - DJ BOOTH - MO-
MENTS LATER

GM is looking through the donation
boxes. GM pulls out a can of tuna.

CALVIN
Most of what I've been living on.

The stores got emptied pretty fast,
but no one thought to check here.

Calvin takes the tuna from GM.

> GM
> I usually just go live in a
> house till I've eaten all their
> food. Then I pack up and move
> across the street. Some of
> these houses are pretty nice.
> Say what you will for the end
> of days, but I've lived in
> worse places.

> CALVIN
> I just miss going out to dinner.

> GM
> Hell, I miss fresh pizza.

A LOUD KNOCK can be heard from outside. GM and Calvin look surprised.

> GM (CONT'D)
> That was fast. Maybe I should
> have wished for two pizzas.

Calvin sticks the tuna in his pocket,
goes to the door to the hall and opens
it slightly.

ANOTHER KNOCK

> GM (CONT'D)
> Does someone know you're here?

> CALVIN
> All my friends are snappers. You?

> GM
> I don't have any friends.

GM pulls out his pistol and slowly
walks down the-

INT. RADIO STATION - HALLWAY - MORNING
- CONTINUOUS

GM and Calvin slowly moving toward the
door.

KNOCK KNOCK KNOCK

Calvin is right behind GM.

GM comes to the door.

> GM
> (yelling out the door)
> Who is it?

> WES (O.S.)

                    (yelling back)
                         GM?

Calvin and GM share a glance.

                         GM
                        Wes?

GM opens the door to Wes, but no Andy.

                         WES
                     It is you!

GM tucks his pistol into the back of
his waistband. Wes walks in and shakes
GM's hand.

                    WES (CONT'D)
            I thought the zombies got you.

                         GM
            Snappers. We call them snappers
              now. Trademark pending.

                         WES
              That's cool. I like that.
                    Snappers.

GM motions toward Calvin.

                         GM

Wes, meet Calvin. Calvin, you
remember the guy I told you I was
hanging with before?

                    CALVIN
            The slow guy?

                    GM
That's the one. So, Wes. What're
you up to these days? What's with
        the orange suit?

                    WES
Oh, I moved into the hospital.

                    CALVIN
        With the crazies?

                    WES
Made some friends. Matter of
            fact…

Wes leans out the door and yells out.

            WES (CONT'D)
            (yelling)
Andy! Come on! Everything's good!

Wes turns to GM.

            WES (CONT'D)

You're gonna like this guy. He's
smart like you.

Andy comes in, a pistol in hand.
He points it right at GM and Calvin.

ANDY
Get them hands up!

Both GM and Calvin are stunned.

ANDY (CONT'D)
UP!

They both put their hands up.

WES
It's okay Andy. I know these
guys.

Wes considers, points at GM.

WES (CONT'D)
Well, I know this one.

Andy looks at GM's name tag.

ANDY
You know Karen? Wait. Karen? What
kinda pussy name is that?

                    GM
              Name's GM.

                  CALVIN
          That's not his shirt.

                   ANDY
      I know guys just like this too.
            Can't be trusted.

                    GM
            (lowering his hands)
                Hey bud-

Andy jams the gun in GM's direction.

                   ANDY
            Get them hands up!

GM stops talking and raises his hands
again.

Andy scoots forward, still aiming the
pistol at them with one hand and pat-
ting Calvin with his other.

He feels something in Calvin's pocket.

                ANDY (CONT'D)
        What is that? Pull it out slow.

                                              145

                    CALVIN
              (as he removes it)
             It's just tuna.

Andy snatches it and looks at it.

                    ANDY
             Good. I like tuna.

Andy sticks the tuna into his pocket,
then turns toward GM and starts pat-
ting him down.
He finds GM's pistol and gives him an
annoyed face while he pulls it out.

                 ANDY (CONT'D)
             Lookie what we have here.

Andy hands the pistol to Wes.

                     GM
             Andy. Is it Andy? I don't think-

                    ANDY
             I told you already to shut up. I
             don't wanna say it again.
                   (to Wes)
             Keep that shooter pointed right
             at'em.

Wes does as he's told.

WES
Sorry GM.

GM
Me too.

ANDY
Looks like Bob's gonna have some
passengers in his ride today.

WES
Maybe we should take them to The
Reverend.

ANDY
Why would we wanna do that? Let's
just blow'em up and be done with
them?

WES
Reverend says everyone has a
purpose.

CALVIN
That sounds fair, right? Meet
with your reverend and talk?

WES
Plus, you could show Reverend how
you did good. Took
responsibility.

                          ANDY
              Yeah. Yeah. I like that.

Andy waves toward the door.

                     ANDY (CONT'D)
              Alright you two. Saddle up.

EXT. RADIO STATION - PARKING LOT - DAY
- CONTINUOUS

GM and Calvin are being marched out to
their car, Andy and Wes with guns
right behind them.

The convertible top is up.

GM and Calvin share a glance.

                          ANDY
                  No funny business.

They get to Calvin's convertible.

                     ANDY (CONT'D)
                  Karen. You drive.

Andy opens the back door and sees Mr.
Bear strapped in, wearing the shades
next to GM's bag.

                    ANDY (CONT'D)
                  What the hell?

Andy starts laughing and pulls the
bear out. He holds it toward Calvin.

                    ANDY (CONT'D)
                  (making a voice)
          Check me out! I'm a stupid bear!

                    CALVIN
                  (annoyed)
          That's not the bear's voice.

                    ANDY
                  (giving a look)
                  Get in.

GM and Calvin climb in the front, GM
behind the wheel.

Andy tucks Mr. Bear into his belt and
he and Wes climb into the back.

INT. CALVIN'S CONVERTIBLE - STATION -
DAY - CONTINUOUS

The keys are in the ignition.

GM starts it up.

Andy notices GM's bag and peeks
inside.

                    ANDY
          Holy shit. This thing has a
               buncha fun toys.

Andy pulls out the music player and
looks at it.

                ANDY (CONT'D)
          Can't wait to play with this
                    baby.

                    WES
          How about we put the top down.

Andy throws the player back into
the bag.

                    ANDY
               I like that.

Andy waves his gun at GM.

                ANDY (CONT'D)
          Miss Daisy. Put the top down.

                    GM
          If I'm the one driving, that
          makes you Miss Daisy. I'd be

Morgan Freeman.

WES
I think he's right.

ANDY
I don't care who's who. I want
the damn top down.

GM looks around for the button, not
sure what to press. Calvin points the
button out.

CALVIN
That one.

GM
Seems obvious now.

ANDY
You two keep it down.

GM hits the button and the top comes
down.

ANDY (CONT'D)
This is what it's all about.

Andy folds his hands behind his head.

ANDY (CONT'D)

          Karen. Get us moving.

                    GM
              (under his breath)
          Right away Miss Daisy.

EXT. MENTAL HEALTH FACILITY - DAY -
MOMENTS LATER

The convertible pulls up to the gates
to find NEW BOB, a woman wearing the
orange suit, sitting at the guard
booth. New Bob is armed, and Calvin
and GM take note of it.

                    ANDY
              (yelling at the booth)
          New Bob! Open the gate!

                    NEW BOB
              (yelling back)
          The Reverend wants to see you
          Andy.

                    WES
          Ah shit.

                    ANDY
          Well open the damn gate, New Bob!

New Bob hits a button and the gate

slides open. GM pulls into a parking
lot inside.

                    GM
          So just park anywhere…or…?

                   ANDY
          Just not in a handicap spot. I
          hate when assholes park in the
                handicap spots.

In the parking lot are several people,
all in the orange jumpsuits going
about their day. Some are sitting and
talking like they're between classes
in the quad at college. There's also a
large woman wandering about. And not
only is she large, but wearing long
bunny ears, has a little cotton tail,
and is carrying a plastic carrot.

As GM parks, not in a handicap spot,
the large BUNNY WOMAN "hops" to
Calvin's window. Large fake front
teeth stick out like a rabbit.

She stands nearby, waiting with anticipation as everyone gets out of the
car and gathers.

                BUNNY WOMAN

I'm a bunny.

CALVIN
(not sure how to react)
I can see that.

GM
You got the tail and everything.

ANDY
Stay away from my prisoners.

Bunny Woman makes a sad face and "hops" away.

ANDY (CONT'D)
(to our guys)
She ain't really a bunny, ya
know.
(to Wes)
Wes, grab that bag of toys.

WES
That's fine, but I'm gonna wait
outside. Reverend might be in one
of his moods.

Wes grabs the bag as GM leans close to
Calvin.

GM

> I'm going to go ahead and wish
> you a Merry Christmas now,
> because I'm pretty sure we're
> boned.

INT. FACILITY - REVEREND'S OFFICE -
DAY - MOMENTS LATER

The office is surprisingly inviting.
Color on the walls. Plants which have
been cared for are sprinkled around. A
large desk with cozy chairs on the
guest side, with a large leather chair
for the REVEREND.

Reverend is watering one of the plants
with an empty can that once held baked
beans. He seems in good spirits, even
HUMMING a little with the CHRISTIAN
MUSIC being played.

There's a man, an OVERLY ARMED GUARD,
standing in the background. Reverend's
personal bodyguard. He's wearing large
cop shades, even though he's inside.
He's armed, and then some. A gun
hanging from each hip, one strapped
across his chest, and holding a
shotgun propped on his shoulder.

The DOOR SWINGS OPEN and in comes
Andy, GM and Calvin in front.

                    ANDY
        They said you wanted to see…

Andy stops talking as the Reverend
turns and looks at him.

The Reverend smiles, points at the
three of them, twirls his finger and
motions toward the door.

Andy looks at him confused.

                ANDY (CONT'D)
            Are you…?

Reverend points again. And again
twirls his finger.

Calvin and GM look at each other for
answers, and in desperation even look
to Andy who is not much help.

                ANDY (CONT'D)
        You want us to spin around?

                  REVEREND
        I'd like you to all go back
            outside, and try again.

ANDY
Try again?

REVEREND
And knock this time.

Andy starts to protest but instead
turns and walks toward the door.

He looks back and sees Calvin and GM
are both still standing there.

ANDY
Well, you heard him. We gotta go
back out.

Andy grabs GM and Calvin and leads
them outside of the door. Andy KNOCKS
and opens the door.

ANDY (CONT'D)
Can we come in?

REVEREND
Who is it?

ANDY
You know who it is. You can
see me.

REVEREND

Who is it?

Andy makes a face.

ANDY
It's Andy. A guy named Karen…

GM
(talking over Andy)
My name's not Karen.

ANDY
And…umm…

Andy turns to Calvin.

ANDY (CONT'D)
You got a name?

CALVIN
Do I have a name? You think I
just don't have a name?

Andy's tired of waiting for an answer.

ANDY
And they call this guy Tuna.

CALVIN
Tuna?
(to Reverend)

My name is Calvin. And his name
is GM.

REVEREND
Come in! Come in!

The three shuffle in and Andy directs
Calvin and GM to take seats in front
of the Reverend's desk.

The Reverend finishes watering his
plant, sets down the can and takes his
own seat at the desk.

REVEREND (CONT'D)
Welcome children. Welcome to the
house of the Lord.

CALVIN
Didn't know the Lord was so big
on guns.

REVEREND
His angels carried swords. Did
Jesus not run the money changers
from the temple?

GM
With a knotted cord.

GM points at the guard.

GM (CONT'D)
We just never pictured him armed
to the teeth, I guess.

ANDY
I found these two while I was out
laying our dear departed Bob to
rest.

REVEREND
Bless his soul.

ANDY
Bless his soul.

The Reverend studies them a moment.

REVEREND
The Lord above told me he would
provide able souls to help with
tonight's services.

GM
He did?

REVEREND
He did.

CALVIN
(nervous)

I'm sure we can lend a hand and
then get right out of your way.

The Reverend just grins.

> GM
> (nervous and chatty)
> That works for me. Sure. I'm not
> doing anything at the moment.
> Always happy to help out. Just
> ask Calvin here.

> REVEREND
> You two seem stricken with worry.

> GM
> Between Andy and Wes—

> REVEREND
> (surprised)
> Wes was there?

> ANDY
> He was just helping me with Bob.

Reverend studies Andy a moment.

> REVEREND
> Andy. I need you on guard duty
> after service tonight.

                    ANDY
          Again? Awww man, I don't-

The Reverend slaps the desk hard with
his hand and stands up. He doesn't say
a word, but his face says plenty.

Andy turns and starts for the door.

                ANDY (CONT'D)
                (to himself)
     I swear, if I could kill Bob all
          over again, I would.

And Andy's gone.

Sweetness washes back over the Reverend and he sits down. He takes a moment to gather his thoughts and-

                  REVEREND
             You were saying?

GM shakes his head.

                    GM
          Lost my train of thought.

                  REVEREND
     You both have nothing to fear. We
     never hurt anyone...unless the Lord

commands us to; though sometimes
He does.

CALVIN
What does that mean?

REVEREND
He speaks to me and sometimes
through me.

GM
Has He ever mentioned anything
about the snappers out there?

REVEREND
Snappers, you say? I do like
that.

GM
Just sort of a joke.

REVEREND
He has told me, the "snappers,"
as you call them, are back from
hell. God has sent them to
cleanse the Earth.

CALVIN
But why?

REVEREND

Because of the filth of sin on
every single one of us. Have you
even been redeemed?

GM
(happy to speak up)
I was baptized.

REVEREND
In blood?

GM
Water, but it was representative.

REVEREND
Representation isn't worth shit.

A beat.

REVEREND (CONT'D)
You both are like the others
we've come across. Unholy, and
full of deceit. Agents of Satan
himself.

CALVIN
Well, hang on. We're just normal
guys.

REVEREND
Normal? Ever since they locked

the doors on us, they've wanted
us to be… normal.

CALVIN
I didn't mean-

REVEREND
Does that make sense to you? As
if something was normal, we'd
have to do what comes unnaturally
to be it.

Calvin and GM both have no answer.

REVEREND (CONT'D)
No, my children. My brothers and
sisters here know what you mean
by normal. We've stood shoulder
to shoulder and faced that
persecution, right up until the
holy event. And our friend back
there…

The Reverend points at the overly
armed guard. The Overly Armed Guard
gives a little wave.

OVERLY ARMED GUARD
Hey.

REVEREND

...with guidance from the Lord,
opened all the cells to free us
from this oppressive little box
of what is, and isn't normal.
Freed us literally, and
spiritually.

GM
We're both fans of freedom of
religion. And I'd think it's safe
to say we wouldn't ever want you
to feel oppressed.

REVEREND
Let me tell you of oppressed.
They locked us all away. And for
what? For what God lead us to do
naturally? I thought for a moment
the Lord had abandoned me when I
needed Him most, but I should
have known He had a bigger plan.
He lead us here because this is
where it all ends. Where we
present the Lord and His servants
with wine and wafer. And not some
grape juice and cracker. Real
blood. And flesh. Did Abraham not
offer up his own son for
sacrifice?

GM

But God called that back, and He
doesn't really do that any more.
People just take a day or two off
and skip a meal or something.

The Reverend takes GM's response personally.

REVEREND
We are doing as the Lord tells me
to do. Without His light, I was a
sinner. A murderer. A robber. A
buyer of foreign products and a
seller of used cars. But now,
with His guidance, He has set me
free to lead these good people,
and I won't have the likes of you
two, telling me what is, and
isn't...normal.

CALVIN
I think we're getting away from
our message here. We just want to
help you spread the Good Word.

REVEREND
Oh you do, now?

Calvin and GM both nod.

REVEREND (CONT'D)

Insincerity has a smell about it.

The Reverend takes a big sniff.

> REVEREND (CONT'D)
> And you both stink of it.

Reverend looks at Overly Armed Guard.

> REVEREND (CONT'D)
> Take them to the confession
> booth.

Overly Armed Guard steps forward,
grabbing them by the arms and lifting
them both from the chairs.

INT. FACILITY - CELL - EVENING -
LATER

A barred cell with not a lot in it except a barred window to match.

There's a bed which is not in the
greatest shape and a chair pushed
against a small table shoved into the
corner. It is stacked high with bibles
in an array of colors, shapes, and
varying conditions.

GM and Calvin are pushed into the cell

by the Overly Armed Guard before he
locks it behind them and leaves.

GM
This is a confession booth?

Calvin starts looking around the cell.

GM strolls over to the window and
peers out.

GM (CONT'D)
Beautiful view of nothing out
here if you're interested.

Calvin keeps shuffling around, pulling
up the mattress.

GM (CONT'D)
What are you doing?

CALVIN
Looking for something to fight
with.

Calvin points at the chair and starts
walking towards it.

CALVIN (CONT'D)
We could pull the chair legs off
and hit them with it.

                    GM
     Gun against chair leg's going to
     be a short fight. Guess who wins.

                    CALVIN
          Well, it's something.

                    GM
        It's hardly got the edge over
              harsh language.

Calvin goes back to shuffling, hitting
a stack of bibles and they topple like
a house of cards.

Behind the stack, a man's head. Its eyes
shoot open and the mouth starts biting.
Calvin jumps back.

                    CALVIN
          Jesus fuck, what is that?

                    GM
        Pretty sure that's a head.

                    CALVIN
              Is it real?

                    GM
     You think it's just a decoration?

(sarcastic)
You have Christmas all year and
they have Halloween. Sure.

Calvin picks up one of the bibles and
reaches out and pokes the head.

The head looks at Calvin, still biting
at him.

The door CLANGS open surprising Calvin
and GM. It's Andy, and he's pointing
his pistol. Mr. Bear still tucked in
his belt.

Calvin sees Mr. Bear and points.

CALVIN
Give me back Mr. Bear.

ANDY
I got your bear AND your tuna
fish.

GM
You can have them. We just
need to-

Andy whacks GM across the face with
the pistol, knocking him to the

171

ground, and then pointing it right
at him.

                    ANDY
    You shut up! You think it's funny
        to tell on me to The Reverend?
    Andy has a wild look in his eye.

Calvin takes a step toward him, but
Andy's on him. He points it at Calvin
and Calvin freezes.

Wes rushes in and grabs Andy's arm.

                    WES
    Andy! We can't do that! They're
            needed at the service.

Andy gives all three a look and then
leaves in a huff. Once Andy has gone,
he looks at GM.

                WES (CONT'D)
    Don't worry. I'm gonna help you
                guys.

                    CALVIN
                Oh thank God.

Wes sees the head.

                    WES
        You found Todd! I been looking
                for him.

Wes walks over and picks up Todd by
his hair. The head snaps at the air.

                  CALVIN
        You said you were gonna help us?

                    GM
          Yeah. What's the plan?

Wes sets Todd down and reaches into
his pocket and pulls out a bottle of
water.

He unscrews the cap and then whips the
bottle hitting GM with water, and then
Calvin.

                    WES
        There. You supposed to die better
            now that you baptized.

Calvin and GM are both in shock as Wes
sticks the bottle back into his
pocket, picks up Todd, and then steps
outside the cell pulling the door
shut.

GM and Calvin are once again alone.
Calvin wipes the water from his face.
GM plops down on the bed.

                    GM
    If you have any ideas, I am allll
            ears right now.

Calvin goes to the window and looks
out. He sees something.

                GM (CONT'D)
        Told you. Beautiful view of
                nothing.

Calvin can't look away. GM stands and
starts walking over.

                GM (CONT'D)
        Whatever you are seeing, it
                can't be…

Multiple snappers all being lead into
the building, all chained together
like a chain gang.

New Bob is in the front leading them
by their chain, Bunny Woman in the
back with a chain as well, keeping the
line taut.

They CLANK and SHUFFLE and MOAN and
ZAP as they pass by the window.

Calvin and GM can't look away.

> CALVIN
> Like cattle.

> GM
> Hungry cattle.

INT. FACILITY - AUDITORIUM - EVENING -
LATER

Rows of orange jump-suited men and
women line the seats of the auditorium, seats on either side of an isle.
They're standing in front of their
chairs, all holding hymn books,
singing "Are You Washed In The Blood."
And they sound beautiful.

The section of the front row is suspiciously empty, with steel reinforce-
ments on either side.

In front of the singing choir is a woman
leading the ceremony from a pulpit on a
raised stage, and she's keeping the
beat with her arms, conducting.

Near the stage is GM's bag.

In the back are the main doors.
Crudely built cages with little pens
on either side, jam packed with
snappers.

As the song goes on, The Reverend en-
ters from those large doors. He's
feeling the music in his soul as he
makes his way down the aisle. Dancing
a little. Singing a little. He lives
for this.

He reaches the pulpit and gives the
CONDUCTING WOMAN a look of admiration,
which she returns without missing a
beat.

The song comes to an end and The Reverend helps Conducting Woman from the
stage, down to her seat.

The front section remains empty.

The Reverend steps up to the pulpit
with a smile.

                    REVEREND
          Brothers and sisters. Take your
                     seats.

The congregation all sit.

>   REVEREND (CONT'D)
>   I speak to you today of Paul, and
>   his letter to the Corinthians.
>   The Lord said, "Though our outer
>   self is wasting away, our inner
>   self is renewed day by day. For
>   this light momentary affliction
>   is preparing for us an eternal
>   weight of glory beyond
>   comparison."

The Reverend starts to walk around on
the stage, becoming very animated with
every word.

>   REVEREND (CONT'D)
>   "Though I walk through the
>   darkest valley, I will fear no
>   evil."

Reverend looks out at his people, and
then points skyward.

>   REVEREND (CONT'D)
>   "For Thou art with me."

The audience APPLAUD AND HOOT.

The Reverend soaks this in as he makes
his way back to the pulpit.

He reaches down and pulls out a rifle
with one hand, and a bat with the
other.

> REVEREND (CONT'D)
> My rod…

He holds up the rifle.

> REVEREND (CONT'D)
> And my staff…

He holds up the bat.

> REVEREND (CONT'D)
> They comfort me.

He uses them to make a cross, and
holds it toward the crowd.

Again, the crowd loves it. And again,
The Reverend can't get enough.

Overly Armed Guard joins him on the
stage and takes them from The Reverend.

> REVEREND (CONT'D)

> (to Overly Armed Guard)
> Thank you my son.

Overly Armed Guard climbs off the
stage.

> REVEREND (CONT'D)
> We gather here today to speak of
> the bidding of the Lord.

The chain gang of snappers we saw before CLANK AND MOAN their way into the
room, heading to the front row.

New Bob still leading the pack with
Bunny Woman bringing up the rear.

> REVEREND (CONT'D)
> As our Savior was resurrected, so
> have these people who were as
> dead as dead can be and were
> even, for a moment, witnesses to
> the fires of hell.

The Reverend makes his way off the
stage as Bunny Woman and New Bob lock
the chains down on the reenforced
steel on the front chairs, locking
them into place, and then take their
spots standing nearby.

The snappers don't really sit in the
chairs, but are in them, more or less.

> REVEREND (CONT'D)
> But they have come back. Yes
> they've come back and been given
> another chance and let us know
> they are of the Lord and to see
> that life is eternal. Can I get
> an Amen?

> CONGREGATION
> AMEN!

The Reverend comes down to the front
row and is speaking to the snappers as
well as the living.

> REVEREND
> We must not ignore their need to
> feed. For to do so would be to
> ignore the very will of the Lord.
> They are hungry sheep, and we are
> their shepherds under the
> watchful eye of the Great
> Almighty Shepherd. And we must
> provide for these souls who can
> not easily provide for
> themselves.

More applause. A beat.

REVEREND (CONT'D)
And I'm happy to say, as he
always does, the Lord has indeed
provided.
(yelling out of the room)
Bring'em in, boys!

The back doors swing open and GM and
Calvin are marched into the room by
Andy and Wes at gunpoint. Wes takes a
seat at the back of the congregation
as Andy takes our guys onto the stage.
Calvin and GM notice the bag nearby.

REVEREND (CONT'D)
It's a special service tonight.
For the Lord has lead these two
unholy deceivers right to our
door. These two soon to become
tonight's…

He pauses for effect.

REVEREND (CONT'D)
WINE AND WAFER!

The Reverend points at GM and Calvin
as the congregation goes nuts. Applause and hoots.

ANDY

(to Calvin)
You and Karen here about to get a
big dose of the Jesus.

The Conducting Woman stands and again
takes to the stage.

The congregation all rise, hymn books
in hand.

Conducting Woman starts them off again
with WASHED IN THE BLOOD, and the congregation follows sounding like an an-
gelic choir.

Calvin knows this is the last moment
to make a move. His eyes dart around,
looking for the escape.

Calvin pushes Andy backwards and GM
follows his lead grabbing at
Andy's gun.

Calvin heads for GM's bag while GM
grabs and wrestles with him.

The sound of the beautiful chorus ring
out from the congregation as Calvin
picks up the bag…but Wes is there.

Wes and Calvin play a tug-a-war with

the bag, Calvin trying to hold the bag
and reach inside.

GM kicks at Andy, catching him right
in the little snapper. Andy buckles,
but still doesn't release the gun.

The congregation one-by-one come to a
stop turning their attention away from
the Conducting Woman and instead to
Calvin.

Calvin is still tugging at the bag,
fishing around inside for anything.

His hand finds something and he pulls
it out. The portable speaker.

Wes does a final yank, pulling the bag
free of Calvin's hands.

                    REVEREND
        Oh son. There's no changing the
              will of the Lord.

                    CALVIN
        Then let's give Him something to
                  dance to.

Calvin hits the button on the player,
and the DEAD BEAT from the rooftop

starts up.

The snappers on the front row all
stand, pulling at the chain together.

Bunny Woman and New Bob grab at the
chains as they continue to pull free,
yanking them around.

Calvin holds the player above his
head.
The snappers start to jive, and the
chain pops free.

The snappers are feeling it, getting
closer to the Reverend as they head
toward the music.

                    WES
        See! I told ya! They dance!

Andy has forgotten about our guys,
stepping forward to see the undead
mosh pit that's formed.

The Reverend is already looking for a
way to spin this.

The Reverend reaches out and touches
the snappers who are too busy dancing
to notice.

REVEREND

You see? God protects me even now
from their hunger.

The Reverend smiles as he looks
across the congregation all starting
to nod and agree. Then he turns toward Calvin whose smile is even bigger, and the Reverend's twinkle
starts to fade.

REVEREND (CONT'D)
What are you…

Calvin hits a BUTTON on the player and
the MUSIC STOPS.

The snapper party stops, and the
hunger begins. Eyes ZAP and they turn
to their nearest meal; The Reverend.

They jump on him like fat kids on the
last piece of cake.

The Reverend is knocked to the ground,
almost lost in a sea of snapper bodies, CLAWING, BITING, SNAPPING, and
ZAPPING.

And just before he vanishes into the
masses he screams:

                REVEREND (CONT'D)
                GOD DAMN IT!

And he's gone, lost in the CHEWING
NOISES.

GM looks around, but Andy is gone. He
has no intention of being stuck with
the check.

GM spots him headed for the large
doors in the back. Andy swings open
the pens at the back and more snappers
start to pile out.

Wes sees Andy has bailed.

                     WES
                    Andy!

But he's gone. Out the back doors, a
sea of undead between them.

Snappers start to swarm the congregation causing everyone to scatter. They
quickly forget their love for the
snappers as the realization sets in
they've ended up on the buffet.

The congregation all start trying to

fend off the snappers swinging their
hymn books at them.

The DEAD BEAT RETURNS.

Calvin is holding the player again,
and the snapper party jumps back off,
parts of the Reverend and some of the
congregation still hanging from their
teeth.

The congregation have no idea what to
do next.

The snappers keep getting closer and
closer to the music. GM jumps off the
stage and grabs the player.

                    GM
     They'll stay with the music. Just
                 leave it.

Calvin sets it on the end of the
stage, the snappers gathering around
it as they feel the groove.

GM walks over to Wes who is in shock,
and yanks the bag from his hands. He
reaches in and grabs pistols from the
bag, handing one to Calvin, tucking

one in his waistband, and gripping
another.

The two of them start making their way
through the gyrating corpses trying
not to touch anyone.

As they limbo and squeeze through,
they see some of the congregation
dancing with snappers.

Maybe it's their disconnection with
reality. Maybe they're just happy not
to be lunch. But they seem to be enjoying the moment.

Calvin is right in the middle of a
large crowd of snappers as the music
starts slowing down, trying to die.

Calvin looks to GM.

                    GM (CONT'D)
        I never charged the damn thing.
                We gotta go.

Calvin not moving.

GM pulls the pistol and fires through
the head of one of the snappers
near him.

                    GM (CONT'D)
                      NOW!

They start scrambling fast.

Carnage is breaking out as the MUSIC
FINALLY GRINDS TO A STOP. The party is
over and the feast has begun.

Entrails are pulled. Blood on
everything.

Snappers ZAP and leap at our guys as
they push them away heading toward the
doors.

GM is shooting at any rotting mass
that moves dropping them as fast as
they come up. Headshot after headshot,
snappers dropping. Calvin is following
in his wake, but not firing.

A snapper wearing the chains almost
gets Calvin, grabbing his arm when
Bunny Woman yanks it back by the
chain.

The snapper leaps on Bunny Woman instead letting Calvin get away.

GM points at one snapper and his gun

CLICKS. Empty. He throws it, bouncing
it off his head and into the crowd.
The snapper pauses, ZAPS, and then
again lunges toward them.

GM picks up one of the congregation's
chairs and swings, hitting a home run,
knocking snapper head sailing.

Another snapper rushes right at him and
he ducks as the snapper goes over the
top of him, knocking it off balance and
GM stands, launching it up and over.

GM pulls the pistol from his belt and
executes the tripped snapper. He
pushes through a crowd of them between
him and the door.

Calvin still following behind, being
no help.

GM looks back at Calvin and two snappers appear suddenly, tackling GM to
the ground.

GM's lost in the pile. Calvin points
his pistol and aims it. He hesitates.

BLAM BLAM. Gunshots. GM pushes limp

snappers off him. But it wasn't
Calvin. It was Wes. He's joined them.

Calvin helps GM to his feet and the
two scramble through the last couple
snappers between them and the door.

Wes grabs GM's bag. Only he's not
after the bag.

> WES
> Take me with you.

> GM
> Let go of the bag!

Wes does.

> WES
> Please help me.

> GM
> Oh, I'll help you like you
> helped me.

GM goes out the door, shutting it behind him leaving Wes looking stunned.

Wes jumps at the door and pulls on the
handles, but they won't open.

INT. FACILITY - HALLWAY - NIGHT - CON-
TINUOUS

GM is holding the doors shut.

He looks at Calvin.

                    GM
          He brought that on himself.

                    WES (O.S.)
                 Help me!

                    CALVIN
               He did help.

Calvin looking at him. GM's torn. Finally it gets the better of him.

                    GM
               Goddamn it.

INT. FACILITY - AUDITORIUM - NIGHT -
CONTINUOUS

Wes is still beating on the doors.

Snappers getting close.

The door opens and GM reaches in and

yanks Wes through, but the sea of
snappers is right there also.

INT. FACILITY - HALLWAY - NIGHT - CON-
TINUOUS

GM tries to shut the door behind him,
but it's too late. The snappers have
breached. Undead arms swing around inside like an unmanned fire hoses.

A crawling snapper, everything missing
from the waist down, reaches out at
GM's legs and finds purchase. It pulls
GM down.

GM falls and the door bursts open.

Calvin and Wes are trying to get it
closed again, both of them holding
back the tsunami of the damned.

Calvin still doesn't want to shoot,
but he's swinging his pistol, hitting
them, knocking them back through the
door.

Calvin sees the snapper on GM. GM
kicking with everything he can as it
holds on his other leg.

Calvin points the pistol.

A slight hesitation.

BLAM. A GUNSHOT.

This time, it was Calvin.

The snapper on GM stops moving, and GM
sheds it off. GM jumps up and the
three almost have the door shut.

Two of the snapper's arms at the door
both manage to snag Wes. There's no
saving him this time. The arms are
pulling him inside. Wes is done for.

Wes's SCREAMS echo through the hall as
Calvin pulls the door shut. He holds
the door as he's looking around for
something to jam into the handles.

GM rips off the sleeve of his shirt,
and uses it to tie the door handles
together.

The snappers are SLAMMING against the
door. It won't hold much longer.

                    CALVIN
          We gotta get out of here.

Calvin starts hurriedly moving down
the hall, and he looks back and
sees GM.

He's walking slow. The weight of the
world on his mind.

> CALVIN (CONT'D)
> Come on!

GM sees a chair there against the
wall and he walks over to it and
grabs it.

The door bulges. There's not much time
before they get through.

> CALVIN (CONT'D)
> The door won't hold.

GM sets the chair down in the middle
of the hallway, facing the door.

> CALVIN (CONT'D)
> Come on!

> GM
> Not this time.

And then Calvin sees it. A fresh bite
on GM's leg.

> CALVIN
> Ahh, shit.

> GM
> Ahh, shit is right. But nothing
> to be done now. It is what
> it is.

> CALVIN
> We could cut off the leg maybe.

GM looks at Calvin, appalled.

> GM
> As appealing as that sounds, no.

> CALVIN
> We can figure something out.

The door strains. There's not much
holding it in place but a couple
toothpicks worth of wood.

> GM
> Look kid. I'm not leaving this
> chair. And I don't want to be
> chained up at your house eating
> dog food with your wife bringing
> in the New Year.

> CALVIN

You're just going to sit here in
this chair?

GM reaches into his bag and pulls out
a grenade.

                    GM
        I told you. I always have a
                 plan B.

                  CALVIN
          I can't just leave you.

GM holds the grenade's lever down as
he pulls the pin.

                    GM
        Well, you can stay if you want,
          but it's about to get really
                    loud.

The door finally breaks. Snappers are
headed their way.

Calvin's stunned. He takes a few steps
away. He knows he has to go.

                  CALVIN
         I don't know what to say.

GM lifts his 3-D glasses and puts them

on, staring at his fate as it shambles
down the hall toward him.

                    GM
    You need to learn to say goodbye.

Calvin takes off, heading out the far
door. The snappers start to surround
GM.

GM lets the lever on the grenade fly.

EXT. FACILITY - PARKING LOT - NIGHT -
CONTINUOUS

Calvin is outside where his convertible is parked.

Calvin's hardly out the door when an
EXPLOSION blows the door open and
glass out of the nearby windows,
quickly replaced by smoke.

The explosion causes Andy's head to
poke up from the front seat of
Calvin's vehicle.
Andy sees the carnage and smoke, and
then sees Calvin, ducking his head
back down.

INT. CALVIN'S CONVERTIBLE - FACILITY -
NIGHT - CONTINUOUS

The steering column wires are exposed
and Andy is trying to make something
happen with little success.

> ANDY
> (mumbling to himself)
> You always make this look so
> easy.

> CALVIN (O.S.)
> (yelling)
> Andy!

Andy pokes his head back up and sees
Calvin standing outside, aiming his
pistol at the car.

EXT. FACILITY - PARKING LOT - NIGHT -
CONTINUOUS

Calvin still pointing his gun at
the car.
Andy ducks out of sight again.

> ANDY (O.S.)
> (yelling out)
> You have the keys?

                    CALVIN
                 (yelling back)
        You're not taking the car. Or the
                    bear.

Andy slides out and then slams the
door shut. Calvin points the gun at
him the entire time.

Andy's pistol is in his holster.

               CALVIN (CONT'D)
          You're not taking the bear.

Andy pulls the bear from his belt.

                    ANDY
        What's with you and this bear?

Calvin doesn't answer.

                ANDY (CONT'D)
        I'm pretty fast, buddy. Alright.
        Have it your way. I'm gonna draw
             on the count of three.

Calvin extends the pistol, pointing
right at Andy.

                ANDY (CONT'D)
          You don't have it in ya…

Calvin looking for the courage.

                    ANDY (CONT'D)
                         One…

Andy's fingers wiggle above the
pistol.

Calvin still looking for the
strength.

                    ANDY (CONT'D)
                         Two…

There's a long pause. The anticipation
builds.

                    ANDY (CONT'D)
                         Three.

Andy is fast. He pulls the pistol up
but like last time, fires early, this
time shooting himself in the leg and
dropping the pistol.

Andy falls to the ground holding his
leg as the blood starts to soak into
the jumpsuit.

Calvin has a moment of relief. He
never fired a shot.

Calvin walks over to Andy and kicks
his pistol far away, then stands over
Andy.

                    CALVIN
              Give me the bear.

Calvin sticks his hand out.

Andy reluctantly gives it to him as he
works through the pain.

Calvin holds up Mr. Bear and wiggles
him as he talks.

                CALVIN (CONT'D)
                 (as Mr. Bear)
            This is my real voice.

                    ANDY
                  (in pain)
          You're as crazy as these guys.

Smoke is still pouring from the door
and windows of the building.

A noise from the doorway causes Calvin
to turn and look.

It's Snapper Wes. He's found his way
outside and is headed right to Andy

and Calvin.

Calvin gives a little wave to Andy on the ground and starts for the convertible.

> ANDY (CONT'D)
> Don't leave me here.

Andy tries to stand, but can't. He starts crawling after Calvin.

> ANDY (CONT'D)
> Why won't you help me?

Calvin turns around and looks at Andy.

> CALVIN
> Because you are fucking up my Christmas.

Andy looks confused as Calvin climbs into the car.

INT. CALVIN'S CONVERTIBLE - FACILITY - NIGHT - CONTINUOUS

Calvin seatbelts in Mr. Bear and puts the shades on him.

Calvin pops open the glove box, pulls

out a spare key and uses it to start
the ignition.

Out the window, Andy is still crawling
closer, leaving a trail of red like a
slug. Wes is gaining on him.

Calvin turns on the radio to hear his
Christmas music playing.

He has a half-hearted smile.

He throws the car into reverse and
pulls back.

Out the window we see Wes is only moments from having an Andy snack.

Calvin puts it in drive and heads out.

INT. CALVIN'S HOUSE - GARAGE - NIGHT -
LATER

Calvin pulls into the garage.

He's still. Thinking.

EXT. CALVIN'S YARD - NIGHT - CON-
TINUOUS

Calvin is looking at all the decorations in the yard.

He spies GM's Santa hat with the hole in it, still hung on the reindeer.

He picks it up and sticks his finger through the hole.

MONTAGE:

Calvin is now wearing's GM's Santa hat with several shots of him hanging up lights, straightening up Jesi, snowmen, and reindeer. All the decorations he and GM had brought to the yard.

MONTAGE ENDS

Calvin is standing back looking at his work, the angle keeping the final display hidden.

Gathered along the fence are several snappers. Ray included. If it wasn't for the fact they had rot for brains, you'd think they were intrigued by the spectacle.

Calvin looks pleased as Punch.

EXT. CALVIN'S YARD - NIGHT - LATER

Calvin is dressed like he's about to
sit down at Christmas dinner with the
in-laws. He still has on GM's
Santa hat.

Chained to the fence is Ella, the big
cover over her head so Calvin could
get her out here.

Mr. Bear, wearing a little Santa hat
of his own, is sitting nearby on
Tina's mound of dirt.

The lights of the decorations are
still off.

Nearby sit two presents. One a normal
box, another a long thin one, both
with festive bows on top.

The line of snappers has grown in size
crowding around the fence. MOANING and
ZAPPING.

Calvin pulls the cover off Ella,
keeping a safe distance.

                    CALVIN

        Ella sweetheart. I think you're
           going to be proud of me.

He holds a moment, and then flips a
switch connected to all the lights
shining like a landing strip.

We soak in the view of bright colors,
motorized displays moving, and a giant
Santa right in the middle.

                  CALVIN (CONT'D)
                  Oh, and…

Calvin jumps up and hits a button on a
radio he's brought outside.

CHRISTMAS MUSIC in mid song starts
playing.

                  CALVIN (CONT'D)
              Pretty festive, right?

Ella really looks like she's enjoying
it. Maybe somewhere in that dead head,
she knows.

Calvin looks proud.

                  CALVIN (CONT'D)
                     Perfect.

>   Calvin walks over to the tree and
>   grabs the normal box.

>   CALVIN (CONT'D)
>   And, I have the gift you gave me
>   to open here.

He opens the box and finds a tacky
Christmas sweater with the words, "Bah
Humbug," written on it.

>   CALVIN (CONT'D)
>   You know me so well.

He laughs.

He considers.

>   CALVIN (CONT'D)
>   You know what? Let's do it.

Calvin throws on the sweater and
straightens it out, showing it to
Ella.

>   CALVIN (CONT'D)
>   Looks good, right?

Calvin is grinning from ear to ear.
Ella's eyes ZAP.

>   CALVIN (CONT'D)
> And, I got something for you too.
>   I hope it fits.

Calvin picks up the long box and
cracks it open.

We can see inside a shotgun with a
little ribbon tied to it.

>   CALVIN (CONT'D)
>   It's a little hot to…

Calvin sees Ella. If he didn't know
better, he'd think she was really enjoying the lights and everything.

Calvin takes a step behind Ella. He
has the shotgun which he points at the
back of Ella's head.

>   CALVIN (CONT'D)
>   Merry Christmas, sweetheart.

And we pull away from the house, the
LIGHTS TWINKLING, the DEAD MOANING,
and the MUSIC PLAYING.

And we hear the SHOT as we GO BLACK.

A beat.

Calvin can be heard speaking over the darkness...

> CALVIN (O.S.) (CONT'D)
> Merry Christmas you snappers...

BACK TO SCENE

Calvin looking right into the camera holding Mr. Bear, both wearing their respective Santa hats.

> CALVIN (CONT'D)
> (into camera as Mr. Bear)
> ...And to all, a good night.

And like Santa's cookies on Christmas morning, we are GONE.

> MERRY CHRISTMAS

The following pages feature images from the film *Christmas with the Dead*. Used by permission.

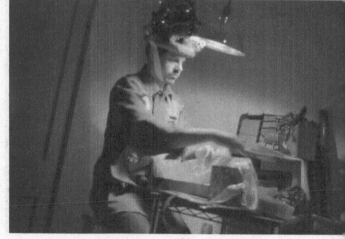

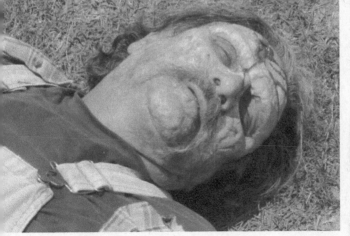

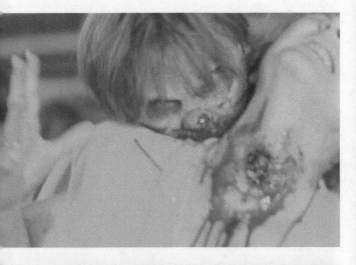

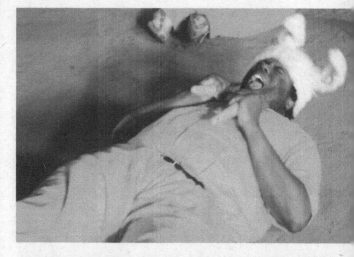

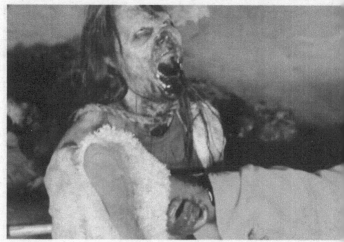

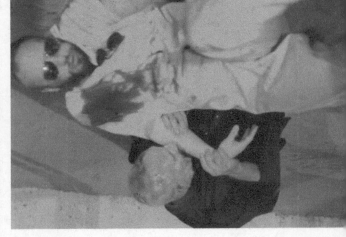